# A Merciful Deception

*Get me out of here,* she'd said.

Giric bit out a silent oath. Saving her had been a foolish notion anyway. What made him think he could do that? His days of rescuing damsels in distress were long over. Now everything he touched he tainted with death.

The lass's fingers tensed subtly within his palm, as if she sensed his unease.

"Ye *have* come to rescue me, haven't ye?" she ventured.

"O' course," he lied, praying he wouldn't live to regret his words.

His mouth curved into a rueful grimace at the thought. He probably wouldn't live at all. And even if he found a way out, he was the last man on earth she should count upon to save her.

THE STORMING
Copyright © 2018 by Glynnis Campbell

Excerpt from BRIDE OF FIRE
Copyright © 2019 by Glynnis Campbell

Cover design by Richard Campbell
Formatting by Author E.M.S.

Glynnis Campbell – Publisher
P.O. Box 341144
Arleta, California 91331
Contact: glynnis@glynnis.net

ISBN-10: 1-63480-039-7
ISBN-13: 978-1-63480-039-6

Published in the United States of America.

# the
# storming

The Prequel Novella to
The Warrior Daughters of Rivenloch

# OTHER BOOKS BY GLYNNIS CAMPBELL

THE WARRIOR MAIDS OF RIVENLOCH
The Shipwreck (novella)
A Yuletide Kiss (short story)
Lady Danger
Captive Heart
Knight's Prize

THE WARRIOR DAUGHTERS OF RIVENLOCH
The Storming (novella)
A Rivenloch Christmas (short story)
Bride of Fire
Bride of Ice
Bride of Mist

THE KNIGHTS OF DE WARE
The Handfasting (novella)
My Champion
My Warrior
My Hero

MEDIEVAL OUTLAWS
The Reiver (novella)
Danger's Kiss
Passion's Exile
Desire's Ransom


THE SCOTTISH LASSES
The Outcast (novella)
MacFarland's Lass
MacAdam's Lass
MacKenzie's Lass


THE CALIFORNIA LEGENDS
Native Gold
Native Wolf
Native Hawk

# ACKNOWLEDGMENTS

Thanks to my sister authors
in the original collection—
Lynn Kurland, Patricia Potter, and Deborah Simmons,
to Elaine English for
her persistence in reclaiming my beloved gem,
and to Alicia Vikander and Hugh Jackman
for their inspiration in the rewrite.

*For Ma and Pa Campbell,*
*who always managed*
*to find a candle in the dark*

# ChAPTER 1

*Scotland-England*
*1136*

"Hurry, m'lady! This way!"

Lady Hilaire Eliot's feet slipped on the slimy steps as she scrambled down the dark, dank passageway, following the bobbling firebrand her maidservant held aloft.

Even here, deep beneath the keep, Hilaire could hear the ominous pounding of the battering ram shuddering the wooden gates and stone walls of the castle.

She breathed a silent prayer. What she attempted was perilous. But what would become of her if she remained behind was far more terrifying.

This way, God willing, if she didn't trip and break her neck along the way, she'd slip out of the tunnel on the outer side of the curtain wall. She'd be halfway through the forest by the time the enemy splintered the door to the inner bailey.

"Please, m'lady!" entreated Martha the maidservant, eyeing Hilaire's harp. "Will ye not leave that cursed thing behind? In another moment—"

The thudding abruptly ceased, heralding the devastation of the outermost gates of the barbican, the first line of defense.

Martha emitted a fretful squeak.

But Hilaire only clutched the instrument closer. She'd been forced to abandon everything else—her home, her family, her friends. She'd be damned if she'd leave her precious harp behind.

She glanced at her shivering servant, who had always been more like an older sister to her. It had been unfair to drag Martha into this. The risk should have been Hilaire's alone.

"Ye go on back, Martha," she said, reaching for the firebrand. "I can make it on my own from here."

But Martha snatched the torch back out of reach and raised her stubborn chin. "I'm not about to desert ye, m'lady."

"'Tisn't your battle."

"I swore I'd keep ye safe. I don't intend to break my vow."

Hilaire shook her head. Martha's loyalty was touching. But there was no need to make her suffer for Hilaire's reckless choices.

"Don't fret, Martha. I'll keep safe, I promise," she insisted with a confidence she didn't quite feel. "Now hand me the torch so I can find my way out."

But Martha wouldn't hear of it. She shook her head once, then turned on her heel and continued down the passage, speaking over her shoulder. "I didn't swear an oath o' loyalty to Lord William just to abandon his daughter at the first sign o' trouble."

Hilaire appreciated Martha's sense of honor, but she doubted very much that Lord William Eliot would approve. He'd likely prefer the maidservant bring his daughter, kicking and screaming, back to the keep.

Ahead the passage narrowed and the stone steps ran out, becoming less a corridor and more a burrow.

Hilaire's pulse raced.

Her legs threatened mutiny.

Usually, Hilaire's daring exceeded her caution. She was as brave as her warrior brothers, as fearless as any of her father's knights. But she had one secret weakness. She hated the dark—closed spaces in particular. Sometimes at night, even the prospect of pissing in the confining garderobe made her heart flutter so much that she'd languish in misery till morning.

This place smelled of mildew and decay, like a grave. She could imagine rats and beetles and worms slithering in the clammy chinks of moldering rock.

Swallowing hard to dislodge the lump of terror in her throat, she forced one foot in front of the other, reminding herself that the tunnel would eventually open up again. If she could endure the harrowing journey for a quarter of an hour, she'd emerge again in the fresh night air.

The passageway had been excavated more than a century ago by her Eliot ancestors, who had lived through constant war. But these were more peaceful times. In all her nineteen years, no one had needed to make use of the tunnel.

If the truth be known, the attack raging above them wasn't even a true battle. It had started as a negotiation—a reasonable refusal to an unreasonable demand.

But her enemy hadn't accepted that refusal. He'd lost his patience. What had begun as a slow siege had become a storming—an assault severe enough to warrant drastic counter-measures.

"Wait!" Hilaire held up a hand, halting Martha. "Did ye hear that?"

The torchlight flickered across Martha's pinched features as she strained her ears. "What, m'lady?"

Hilaire's brow creased in worry. She thought she'd heard...

But perhaps it was only her bones creaking with cold or her knees rattling with fright.

She dismissed her fears with a shake of her head. "We should make haste."

The tunnel angled sharply downward as it passed underneath the curtain wall. Hilaire shuddered.

Creeping down the incline was like descending into a cold hell.

"Mind the—" Martha warned, too late.

Hilaire's toe caught on a tree root. She stumbled and fell hard, landing on both knees in the soil. Her harp struck a discordant *twang* as she caught herself on one hand.

"Oh, m'lady! Are ye hurt?"

Hilaire silently cursed her clumsiness. Thankfully, her nubby woolen skirts had taken the brunt of the fall. Her palm was only bruised. "I'm fine."

But was she?

Here bold and courageous Lady Hilaire Eliot knelt like a pathetic wretch in the cold, dank mud. With nothing but her harp, a peasant's kirtle on her back, and a scared servant, she was fleeing her home and a future she couldn't bear to face. The weight of her circumstances and the depth of her dread pressed down upon her like a millstone.

How had she come to such a coil?

If only Lord William had betrothed her to someone sooner, before the king had the chance to arrange her marriage…

She would have wed anyone her father named— bandy-legged Edmund Beattie, somber Lord Robert of Kinmont, even Sir Simon Duff, who stuttered and walked with a limp—anyone but the monster the king had chosen for her.

People spoke of The Dire Dragan in whispers, for fear that uttering the Highlander's name might call his curse upon them. They claimed his countenance was dark with the shadow of damnation. His hair was as black as char. His eyes were as deep as a chasm. He never smiled, seldom spoke, and when he did, it was in a low growl more akin to an animal than a man.

Once, the pennant of The Dragan had flown proud. Its master, deserting his Highland home for the more civilized Borders, had been graced with the noble qualities of the creature blazoned on his crest—fierce power and a true heart. Once he'd been a warrior of great honor and renown.

But that was long ago.

Now it was said he need only sear a man's eyes with his burning gaze to send him cowering to his knees. The Dragan had become the most horrible of beasts, for he was ferocious, dangerous, and full of deadly fire.

Still, nothing was as terrible as the curse he placed upon women.

To them he brought death.

Three wives he'd already lain in the grave—one beside her young daughter, one with a babe still in her belly, and one before he could even get her with child. Three wives, and not one had borne him a son upon whom to bestow his title.

A woman would have to be mad to wed such a man.

And, by all that was holy, Hilaire was not mad.

Struggling to her feet, she set out with renewed determination.

They'd almost reached the lowest point in the passageway, where the curtain wall was anchored and where the tunnel thankfully ascended, when she heard it again—the sinister creaking of mortar and stone.

"Let me," she said, taking the firebrand from Martha in her free hand and squeezing past the maid to investigate the passage ahead.

The sound came from directly above her now. She turned back for an instant to see if Martha could hear it as well.

Then, with an unholy crack, the sky fell.

Giric mac Leod wiped his damp brow with the back of his sleeve and stabbed at the earth again with his spade, deepening the tunnel. He wondered for the hundredth time if he was doing the right thing.

What kind of fool stormed a bloody castle in the middle of the night, for God's sake?

It was a desperate action. And yet he could think of nothing else to do.

He'd known it was foolish to come. All his instincts told him this cursed wedding was not to be. But he had no choice.

King David of Scotland, on the brink of peace with the king of England, was intent on forging as many alliances as possible along the border. Besides, the king had pointed out, The Dire Dragan was in need of an heir.

Thus, King David had handpicked the mother of that heir—the daughter of an English border lord—and would brook no refusal.

Giric heaved a weary sigh. He wished the king had chosen another bride, one less vehemently unwilling.

He clamped his mouth into a grim line and shoveled the dirt aside.

A less unwilling bride? That was laughable. No woman in her right mind would wed a man like him.

Clenching his jaw, he gouged another wound into the soil and cast the dirt over his shoulder—unintentionally showering the captain of his knights, arriving behind him, with soil.

"God's blood!" Campbell swore, spitting dirt from his mouth. "There ye are! I've been lookin' high and low for ye, m'lord! What the devil d'ye think ye're doin'?"

"Go away." He didn't need nosy Campbell interfering in his affairs.

"Why, ye're sappin' the castle," Campbell said in wonder, standing his ground. "But ye can't undermine the wall, m'lord, not by yourself."

"Begone, I said."

"Are ye daft? There's nothin' to shore it up. Ye haven't got the proper braces," Campbell insisted. "'Tis death to linger here!"

Giric didn't answer his man, only turned and continued shoveling. He might indeed have to sap the castle, but only as a last resort. What he intended was to dig a small passage, just enough to steal in under the curtain wall and claim his bride.

Campbell cursed again. "At least give *me* the spade then. *I* don't have any vassals I'm beholdin' to."

"Nay!" Giric barked over his shoulder, making the torch flicker. "The lady's to be my wife. 'Tis *my* risk."

He kept digging, jabbing at the soil with renewed resolve, punishing the earth for coming between him and his prize.

"But I came to tell ye the barbican's fallen," Campbell said. "Once we penetrate the inner wall—"

"Nay. Delay the attack. Just maintain the siege, and keep Eliot's men distracted."

"But, m'lord, we can easily take the castle by force."

"And slay my bride's kin?" He tossed the spade aside, and dug a small boulder from the embankment with his hands. "Nay. 'Tis far easier to repair the barbican than make amends for slaughter."

"At least let me call the sappers. They'll put up decent props, and in a day or so—"

"I haven't got a day or so," Giric grumbled, casting the stone away. "Besides, 'tis a matter for stealth, not force."

Campbell blew out an exasperated breath. "Ye know, m'lord," he said, his voice as bitter as moldy ale, "if I didn't know better, I'd say ye were itchin' to kiss death's arse."

There was some truth to that. Sometimes Giric didn't feel like he had much to live for.

Then, as if Campbell's words invoked some black doom, the air was suddenly severed by an ominous crack.

Silt sifted down over Giric's head, extinguishing the candlelight. Then an enormous slide of rock and earth pelted him, muting Campbell's shouts and utterly blotting out the night sky behind him.

Hilaire cried out as devil's thunder split the air. But the sound was lost beneath the violent, crashing deluge of ragged stone and fetid soil that sealed the tunnel. Her maid vanished from sight.

Dust filled her nose and mouth, clogging her throat, choking her, and most horrifying of all, smothering the flame of her torch. A brutal impact knocked her forward and sent her sprawling atop her harp. Shards of rock pummeled her back like sharp-sided hail. Then a heavy chunk of stone smashed her hand, and she grunted in pain.

The awful clamor seemed to go on forever, at last diminishing from a roar to a rustle as the boulders came to rest and pebbles continued to trickle down all around her. But as horrible as the noise was, it was not half as terrifying as the deadly silence that followed.

Hilaire struggled to hear anything, anything at all—her maid, a rat, the echo of the battering ram—but her own frantic gasps and the loud rushing of her pulse were the only sounds remaining.

The world had turned absolutely black.

Not the black of a starless night.

Not the black of the dungeon.

Not even the black of the close garderobe that set her heart to hammering.

This was a black so heavy, so tangible, it wrapped like a shroud about her.

She was afraid to get up, afraid she'd find the space around her had shrunk to the size of a coffin. Panic rattled the cage of her mind, and a squeal of dread lodged in her throat. She sucked what breath she could into her lungs, but it was impossibly thin.

Growing dizzy, she forced herself to calm, measuring out her shuddering breaths. If she succumbed to terror, she knew she'd be lost. She had to steel her nerves, get up, and assess her situation.

The harp dug painfully into her stomach, and her hand throbbed where it was caught beneath the rock. The slippery warmth of blood oozed between her crushed fingers. She was trapped.

Nay, she told herself. Nay.

Biting her lip to stave off panic, she brought her knees up under her. She scrabbled through the rubble, digging away the debris. She finally pried the heavy stone up enough to free her trapped hand, hissing between her teeth and cradling the injured member to her breast.

There was no time to lick her wounds. She had to find a way out. There *must* be a way out, she told herself, willing her breath to slow. The tunnel had collapsed between her and her maid. It followed then that she need only proceed forward to find her way to the other end and freedom.

Her pulse pounding in her temples, she groped the walls, looking for the exit, praying for a breach. She hobbled around the cave, stumbling, fumbling, searching. But as she circled the tiny enclosure again and again, she discovered the horrible truth. The falling earth had sealed both sides of the tunnel.

God's bones—she was buried alive.

Breathless with dread, a scream threatening inside her, she retrieved her harp, clutching it to her chest like a drowning man clinging to a timber.

Her first cries were weak and thready, hoarse with fear. But desperation soon moved her to cry out for help at the top of her lungs.

Giric sat stunned. He should be dead. Enough debris had fallen around him to fill a decent-sized moat. But, somehow, God in his infinite mercy—or infinite cruelty—had spared him a quick death.

He'd still die. He had no doubts about that. He'd search every crevice of his new dungeon with the thoroughness of a captive plotting escape from The Tower. But it would be of no use. For when The Dire Dragan set about doing a thing, he did it properly.

The undermining had worked brilliantly. The castle curtain wall had collapsed, if prematurely, precisely as a sapper would have intended. Without the braces, however, Giric was imprisoned by his own hand under tons of rock and rubble.

His mouth twisted with black humor. It seemed he'd accomplished quite an admirable feat. By the complete lack of light, Giric was certain not even a chink remained for the wind to blow through.

Then his heart sank. Campbell. Why hadn't the stubborn Highland captain left when Giric ordered him away? The poor wretch had probably been buried in the collapse. Even if by some miracle Campbell survived and could bring rescue, Giric would suffocate by the time his men could dig through the massive wall of granite.

Meanwhile, Giric would have time to dwell on his sins, to relive all the ugly passages of his life.

A small part of him, deep inside, felt a wrenching sort of satisfaction. After all, this was the end he *deserved.* At last Giric would suffer for his crimes and do penance for the innocent lives he'd destroyed.

And the young woman who waited within the castle walls to be his bride, whose father had stubbornly refused to surrender his maiden daughter in sacrifice to The Dire Dragan? She could stop wringing her hands in terror, for the beast she was betrothed to would be dead in a few hours.

Giric raised his hand to his forehead. His fingers came back slick with blood. He felt the sting of several scrapes and gashes along his bared forearms. All his bones seemed intact, though he was certain he'd be bruised on the morrow.

Then he chuckled bleakly. Bruised! He'd be *dead* on the morrow.

His laugh turned to coughing as the dust settled invisibly around him in the pitch black. Perhaps Campbell was right about him. Perhaps he *had* been courting death, for the idea of dying brought nothing but relief.

No more would he be haunted by the images of his loved ones' lifeless bodies.

No more would men cower as he passed, crossing themselves before him, making the sign of the devil behind his back.

No more would lords' daughters quiver in fear at the prospect of becoming his bride.

Once he paid the debt of his soul, he'd be free.

He gathered dusty saliva in his mouth and spit it onto the ground. The thirst would be the worst of it, he supposed. Aside from that, once the air ran out, he'd likely just drift off to sleep.

No more worries.

No more responsibilities.

No more innocents to harm.

He crossed his battered arms over his chest, closed his eyes against the black oblivion, and gave up the fight, settling back against the jagged rock that would mark his grave.

The repose of eternity lasted exactly five measured breaths.

Then he heard it, faint at first, like the chirp of a cricket.

He opened one eye, as if that would make any difference in the utter dark.

It came again, louder this time, from beyond the inner wall of the tunnel.

He opened the other eye.

The sound was probably just a mouse, injured in the collapse. He hoped it would die soon. He wanted his last moments on earth to be peaceful.

He frowned, squirmed into a more relatively comfortable position, and closed his eyes tighter.

There it came again.

His eyes flew open.

That was no cricket, no mouse. There was something distinctly *human* about the cry.

He swallowed. When the forlorn cry came again, it sent a shudder through him like a battering ram pounding at his heart. There was no mistake. That voice belonged to a woman. And if there was one sound he couldn't ignore, it was the call of a maiden in distress.

# CHAPTER 2

I t hardly seemed fair. Giric had given up his joust with dogged destiny. He'd resigned himself to dying, slipping away in this quiet tomb with nothing but his own thoughts, fading from the wretched world on a serene and silent breath.

But it was not to be.

That voice called to him.

Needed him.

And stronger than his desire to escape into oblivion was his cursed sense of honor. He was a knight. He'd taken certain oaths, sworn to live by certain morals. And paramount was the vow to protect and defend those creatures weaker than he.

Muttering a mild oath, he pushed himself up from the rubble and fumbled his way toward the source of the noise. It was here, from the place he'd been digging before, a patch of bare earth clear of stones. He pressed his ear to the dirt, listening. The despondent cry came again.

He pulled his head back in wonder. As unbelievable as it seemed, there was someone beyond the innermost side of the tunnel. For one mad moment, he wondered if it was the voice of some dark angel of the underworld, calling him to Hades.

He groped about, searching for his spade, till he remembered he'd tossed it aside before the rockslide. He'd have to use something else then.

His fingers clambered over the debris until he located a sharp shard of stone. Hefting it in his hand, he began jabbing determinedly at the soil. While her cries continued, then hopelessly diminished, his efforts at enlarging the hole in the earth were about as effective as a rat gnawing through iron.

He cast the rock aside. The sound had ceased. God's breath—had she fainted? Was she dead? His heart in his throat, he hurled his body against the tunnel, cupped his hands around his mouth, and shouted as loud as he could.

"Hold on!"


Hilaire sat bolt upright, digging her fingers into the carved wood of her harp, every sense strained. Sweet Mary—was that a voice? Or was it only a delusion, part of the phobia that had reduced her to a quivering child? She bit her lip, trying to still her breath to better hear.

And then, blessedly, the voice came again. Relief burst out of her in a sound that was half laugh, half cry.

Someone was adjacent to the passageway.

It didn't seem possible. She was deep underground, and as far as she knew, only one tunnel led from the castle. But possible or not, the muffled voice on the other side of the dirt embankment was real. And it sounded sweeter to her than the strings of her beloved harp.

"Here!" she cried. "I'm here!"

Still clinging to the harp, she dragged herself toward the source of the voice and pressed her cheek against the damp earthen wall.

He called out again, and she answered. Then she set aside her instrument and with her good hand, began clawing like a shrewmouse at the dirt.

The task was difficult. The tunnel was sunk deep in the bowels of the earth, where the soil was more rock than mud. She scraped the pads of her fingers and broke off two of her nails.

But he kept calling to her, encouraging her, and she continued to wear away at the wall till she heard digging on the other side and felt it give beneath her hand.

Breathless with triumph, she scrabbled at the dirt, enlarging the gap inch by inch. Finally, with a ragged sob of victory, she reached through the makeshift burrow and clasped a miracle. A human hand.

A fount of grateful tears squeezed from her eyes and rolled down her cheeks. She sobbed as warm, strong fingers closed around hers.

He didn't speak for a long while, only holding on to her. It felt as if he transferred his strength into her, sustaining her. She neither knew nor cared who he was. He was another human being in the darkness.

The maiden's hand felt small in Giric's, warm and soft and helpless. He'd forgotten how pleasant the touch of a woman was.

His own hand was coarse and callused from battle, no doubt abrasive to her delicate skin. Yet she made no attempt to withdraw. On the contrary, it seemed as if she might never release him.

His throat thickened at the thought.

She wouldn't be clinging to him if she knew who he was. That much was certain.

But at the moment, she clutched his hand as if her life depended upon it. Or her sanity. From her wild sobbing and the sweaty trembling of her fingers, she seemed but a whisper away from complete madness.

He called to her through the gap. "Are ye hurt?"

"My ha—" she began, then shakily amended her reply. "I'll be fine. Only please...get me out o' here."

She said the last in a rush, and he heard fear lurking beneath her polite request. Her voice was light and sweet, yet never had chivalry called to him quite so powerfully.

But his heart caved at her words.

*Get me out of here,* she'd said.

Shite—was she trapped as well? If so—if her prison proved half as impenetrable as his—all his knightly vows, all his heroic efforts, and all his noble intentions couldn't save her.

He bit out a silent oath. Saving her had been a foolish notion anyway. What made him think he could do that? His days of rescuing damsels in distress were long over. Now everything he touched he tainted with death.

The lass's fingers tensed subtly within his palm, as if she sensed his unease.

"Ye *have* come to rescue me, haven't ye?" she ventured.

She sounded so innocent, so vulnerable. He gave her hand a gentle squeeze.

"O' course," he lied, praying he wouldn't live to regret his words.

His mouth curved into a rueful grimace at the thought. He probably wouldn't live at all. And even if he found a way out, he was the last man on earth she should count upon to save her.

Still, he was obliged to try.

It was difficult to extract his fingers from hers. She was very reluctant to let go of him. But giving her hand a final clasp of sustenance, he began scrabbling again at the soil. She scraped at her side of the hole as well until the gap slowly grew enough—inch by arduous inch—to allow him snug passage through.

"Back away," he told her. "I'll come to ye."

His shoulders scraped against the rough stone as he squeezed through and foundered onto the rocky ground like a newborn foal.

"Are ye all right?" she asked.

The lass's fingers brushed across him as she bent near, making accidental contact with his shoulder, his chest, perilously high on his thigh.

His breath caught. When was the last time a woman had touched him there? His nostrils flared for an instant before her hand slipped away again.

"I'm fine," he croaked, shuffling into a crouch.

The situation looked bleak. The air seemed just as dense and black on her side of the wall. Still, he felt compelled to search every inch for chinks in the armor of their prison.

"Do ye have no torch?" she asked. The request was subtly colored by trepidation.

"Nay."

Women always feared the dark. He wondered why. He found the dark to be a great friend—comforting and concealing.

He explored the cavern slowly, meticulously. Alas, the walls yielded no promise. Those surfaces that weren't as impenetrable as chainmail were plated in the rocky refuse of the deluge. He found no weaknesses.

"Should we not go now, sir?"

He winced at her question. How much should he tell her? He wondered how old the lass was. Too young to die, certainly. Never mind that that hadn't stopped death from taking Giric's four-year-old daughter.

"Sir?" A hint of bewilderment touched her words.

Giric knew he wouldn't be able to shield her for long. He hoped she wouldn't burst into hysterics when he divulged the truth of their situation.

Carefully, he groped his way toward her, contacting first her long, soft hair. It hung loose, caressing his questing fingers like a fine silk veil. But by the rough fabric of her kirtle sleeve, he guessed the lass must be a commoner.

He gripped her gently but firmly by the arms. She felt so small, so fragile in his grasp, like a dove. Lord, such a delicate woman might be easily broken. He ran his tongue uneasily across his lower lip.

"It appears there is no..." he began, clearing his throat. "There is no easy way out."

She stiffened beneath his hands, but to her credit, made not a peep of despair. "I see." Her voice was scarcely a whisper. A long silence ensued, violated only by her shuddering breath. Finally she found her voice. "Do ye think... Are we...are we goin' to die?"

Her words—so guileless, so brittle—cut him like the edge of a blade. A fierce longing to protect her welled up suddenly inside of him. How could he burden an innocent damsel with such an awful truth? How could he bring such suffering to her?

In good faith, he could not.

So he lied. "Nay," he said, giving her arms a reassuring pat. "Never fear." He prayed she couldn't detect the forced levity of his voice. "I only said there was no *easy* way out."

Hilaire bit down on her lip. She wouldn't cry. No matter what happened, she wouldn't lose control. This man, whoever he was, was doing his best to comfort her, even if he was a poor liar. She refused to disappoint him by blubbering like a child. She'd be brave.

Still, when she opened her eyes to all that smothering black, it was all she could do not to scream in horror. In her mind's eye, the walls began to shrink, squeezing her lungs until she could draw no breath. She gasped in the stale air, wheezing faster and faster, as she fought the suffocating sensation.

Not enough air.

Not...enough...air.

"Lass," the man ordered, "easy now."

But she couldn't stop. If she stopped breathing, she'd die. Like a drowning animal, she clawed at him in desperation, twining her fists in the folds of his tabard, hanging on for dear life.

He gave her a wee shake. "Slow down. Or ye'll faint. Breathe with me."

"I...I...can't..." The sound was no more than a whispery squeak.

No air.

No. Air.

She scrabbled at his chest.

He tightened his grip on her, almost to the point of pain, shocking her from her panic, and barked the ferocious command inches from her face. "Breathe with me. In!"

He rasped in a breath, and she battled to match his rhythm.

"Out!"

The breath shuddered out of her.

"In!"

She sucked in another draught of air.

"Out!"

She released her breath.

"In!"

They drew in a loud gasp together.

"Out!"

Her breath escaped on a long sigh.

Then they were breathing together, deeply, calmly. Hilaire felt her lungs gradually expand to take in all the air she required. For the moment at least, her fears were eased.

"Ye see?" he said, "There's plenty of air."

Suddenly ashamed of her panic, she slowly untangled her fingers from the man's tabard. "I'm sorry. I—"

"Don't be." The man ran his thumb soothingly over her arm, as if to apologize for his harshness. For the first time, she noticed the soft clink of chainmail and felt the rigid contour of his hauberk beneath her hands. She wondered who he was.

"Thank ye, Sir...?"

He didn't enlighten her. Who was he? Who was her savior?

His hands were rough, the hands of a man accustomed to labor or warfare, as coarse and rugged as his voice. Yet, like his voice, they possessed gentleness and warmth. He smelled of earth and iron and leather. Though she couldn't tell his age or his bearing, he exuded strength and comfort—enough to assuage her fears.

When he didn't reply, she asked, "Ye *are* a knight, aye?"

"Aye," he grunted.

She wondered if she'd seen him before. Because of the growing alliance between Scotland and England, so

many border knights had sworn fealty to her father in the last year, she honestly didn't know them all by name. She vowed, however, if this man somehow managed to get her out of this hellish grave, she'd embroider his name on every kirtle she owned and remember him in her every prayer.

The man released her arms, interrupting her thoughts. "What is this chamber?" he asked. "How did ye come here?"

She flushed, forgetting her own curiosity. The tunnel was a mild embarrassment to her, having been constructed exclusively for the noble family's use.

"'Tis an underground passageway," she admitted. "It leads from the keep to beyond the curtain wall."

"Ye were fleein' the castle?" he asked.

"Mmm." Perhaps it was best not to elaborate.

"Because o' the attack?"

"Aye."

"Were ye alone?"

She bit the inside of her cheek. She didn't know if Martha yet lived, but there was no reason to incriminate her. "Aye."

"Did anyone know ye were here?"

She hesitated.

"Will anyone miss ye?" he persisted.

"Nay. That is, I mean, aye!" She could ill afford to test the man's patience, but deception didn't come easily to her.

"I only want to know," he said evenly, "if anyone will come lookin' for ye."

"Oh." If he'd brought a torch, he'd have seen her cheeks redden in chagrin. "Oh, aye, I suppose they will. At least, I hope so."

Surely Lord William would search for her. On the other hand, he was not especially pleased with her.

Why would he be? Hilaire had brought ruin upon them all.

When her father had first announced the name of her husband-to-be, she'd adamantly refused the marriage.

But Lord William, long a commander of knights, would never allow his daughter to win in a contest of wills.

So she'd tried to use reason. She'd assured him she would accept the *next* husband the king offered.

William had sternly warned her he was not about to be manipulated.

By the time her bridegroom arrived, Hilaire was reduced to begging and pleading with her father to continue resisting the siege so she could escape.

In the end, he'd buckled in the face of her copious tears. But it had been a gruff farewell he'd bid her, replete with reminders of the king's wrath he invoked with his actions and the great risk he invited in countering the forces of The Dire Dragan.

Hilaire shivered. If only the ancient tunnel hadn't crumbled, she'd be safe now beyond the wall, far away from the tempers of unsympathetic men like the king, her father, and The Dire Dragan. Safe from the suffocating darkness that kept creeping in at the edges of her mind...

Nay, she must not think of that.

The man grunted as he struggled to move the rocks and gravel. His low murmur interrupted her thoughts. "He wouldn't have harmed ye, ye know."

"Who?"

"The Dire Dragan."

She shuddered. "I fear ye're mistaken, sir. I heard the blows he thrust upon the outer gate, even from here."

"'Tis not his way to slaughter the defenseless."

She gave a nervous, humorless wee laugh. "Then pray tell what happened to his last three wives and their children."

A long, cold silence met her query. Then the dull thud of rock upon earth resumed as the man began to pound away at the wall.

"Besides," she added defensively, "'tis an easy thing for ye to say. *Ye* aren't betrothed to the monster."

The pounding stopped as suddenly as it had started, and the man's sharp intake of breath seemed to suck all the air from the tunnel.

Hilaire clapped a hand over her mouth. She hadn't meant to reveal herself to him. If, by some miracle, they managed to dig out of the rubble, she intended to continue along the tunnel to freedom, as originally planned. The knight would think of her no more, just bid her good fortune and return to defending her father's castle. No one would be the wiser.

But now—now she'd made a mess of things.

# CHAPTER 3

"**Y**e're...Lady Hilaire?"

The musty air thickened, choking Giric like smoke from a quickly doused fire.

She tried to deny it. "Nay, I..." Then she released a resigned sigh that seemed to blow through his soul. "Aye, I am."

A dozen emotions warred in his head—pain, relief, anger, joy, fear—like knights battling in a fierce melee.

Hilaire.

His betrothed.

This maiden with the sweet voice, the fragrant hair, the tender touch.

This woman who feared the dark and clung to him with the trust of a drowning kitten.

Lord, what would it be like to wake up each morn to such a wife?

He sighed. It was only a fleeting fantasy. They were dying, he reminded himself. There would be no wedding.

Besides, he thought bitterly, she didn't want him. Hell, she'd risked her life to escape The Dire Dragan.

It was another tragedy in a long line of tragedies. And it was stinging salt in his wounds that though he'd scarcely met the lass, he suspected he might have grown to care for her in time.

Yet he was damned to destroy all he held dear. Curse the Fates—he'd probably killed her already. It was his fault they were trapped. It was because of him the tunnel had collapsed.

"Swear ye won't tell the others," she fretted, grabbing at his sleeve.

"The others?"

"My father's knights. Swear ye won't tell them I was runnin' away."

Giric frowned. So the wee vixen had sneaked off, leaving her father and his knights to defend the castle while she made her escape. Yet what else should he expect?

Though Hilaire was of marrying age, he could tell she was barely a woman. The lass had probably never had her heart broken, never stolen a kiss, never bedded a man. The prospect of wedding The Dire Dragon must have seemed like an order of execution.

"God's truth," she said. "I'm ashamed o' my cowardice." Her hand came to rest upon the middle of his chest, too near his heart for comfort. "But don't tell them. When we're free, let me go in peace. Promise me."

He closed his eyes, almost feeling the warmth of her hand through his armor, and groaned inwardly. Even if they managed to survive this ordeal and get out alive, neither of them had control over their destiny. Two kings had commanded this union. She couldn't avoid marriage to the man she feared. No matter where she fled, the forces of the English and Scots would hunt her down. Against her will, she'd be wed to Lord Giric mac Leod. And once married, she'd be subject to the curse of The Dire Dragan.

But none of that mattered at the moment. They were going to die. What mattered was making her last hours peaceful.

So he gave her his word. "I promise."

Her sigh of relief made it worth the lie.

"Now," she said with renewed hope, "if we keep diggin'..."

Giric grimaced.

The stone of the fallen castle wall was too dense and tightly wedged to allow escape through the hole he'd originally tunneled out, and the earthen wall of her secret passage was so hardly compacted, it might as well be rock.

He had nothing to dig with—no spade, no adze, not even a sword. Their bare fingers would wear down to bloody stumps by the time they tunneled out even a yard of earth. Escape was nigh impossible.

But he didn't have the heart to let her know that. Besides, they might as well make the attempt. It would pass the time and prevent her from dwelling on the darkness. Certainly, it would keep his mind off his miserable past. And perhaps it was a blessing that in his final hours he was closeted in shadow with a lass who didn't know him, a lass who had no cause to fear him.

"Shall we try here?" she suggested. The optimism in her voice tugged at his heart.

"Where?"

Her hand wandered along the links of his mail until she grasped his wrist. Her fingers couldn't even close the distance around his forearm, but she tugged him along like an unruly child, finally placing his palm upon a section of damp earth.

He shook his head. If they dug there, they *would* wind up inside the keep eventually—perhaps forty days hence.

"Do ye not wish to escape the castle?" he asked. "'Tis the opposite wall that leads to freedom."

"But if The Dire Dragan..." Her fingers curled anxiously atop his hand. "Ye wouldn't understand." Her troubled whisper brushed his face, perfumed with the faint scent of mint. It was as intoxicating as mead. "If he finds me...if he discovers I was fleein'..."

He scarcely heard her words. The fragrance coming off of her hair, her skin—what was it? Rose? Lavender?

"I won't wed him," she stated in no uncertain terms. "I cannot. He is a brute. Cruel. And dangerous. And evil. Have ye not heard? He murdered his first three wives and—"

"So I've heard!" The words tore from his throat with more force than he'd intended.

With a silent curse, he began jabbing at the soil, using his blunt fingers like daggers. She couldn't know how she tortured him, what pain she dealt him with her careless remarks.

"Perhaps ye think I should be stronger," she muttered, her voice a shade cooler, misunderstanding his outburst. "Ye doubtless expect me to honor my vows as ye honor yours. But I'm not a knight who battles with a sword and a shield. I'm a lass armed only with my wits and my will. I won't sacrifice myself to a monster when—"

"He is not a mons—" To Giric's mortification, his voice broke.

Damn his weak spirit. He thought he'd become inured to such accusations.

He thought he'd grown scaly plate like the armored dragon on his crest.

He thought he could no longer be wounded by mere words.

He was wrong.

His heart plunged in misery, and his eyes stung, weary of aspersions. God's blood—would even his last moments on earth be corrupted by his vile past?

"Ye...ye *know* him," she whispered suddenly with a woman's insight. It wasn't a question. It was an accusation. "Ye *know* The Dire Dragan."

"Nay." He clenched his jaw against foolish self-pity.

In a sense, he spoke the truth. Once he'd known him well. Once Giric mac Leod had been a noble young Highlander with a blade in his hand, the wind at his back, and adventure in his heart. Now The Dire Dragan was a nightmare he was forced to live. Nay, he no longer knew the man who lived in the shell of his body.

"But I've known men like him," he said.

She was quiet for a long while. Then he heard her retreat.

He should have expected as much. Even here in the dark, without the benefit of face or name or reputation, he was capable of inspiring fear in a woman.

"Who are ye?" she finally asked.

"Nobody." He returned to clawing at the mud.

"Ye aren't one o' my father's company at all, are ye?"

"I'm a knight. That's all. I go where I'm called. I fight when I must."

"Do ye have a name?"

He cursed under his breath. "Are ye goin' to help dig us out or ask questions all night?"

A dissonant *twang* sounded suddenly as she recoiled from his harsh words. The lass must have a gittern or a harp. As the jangling chord faded, the silence grew heavy.

Even blind, he could sense the lass's hurt. But that was good. It would keep her away from him, keep her safe from his evil, keep him bastioned from her charms.

But as the silence dragged on, he heaved a contrite sigh. If one weapon could lay him low in a single blow, it was the knowledge he'd hurt a woman. He chewed at his lip in remorse.

"Forgive my rough manners." After several moments, she still hadn't spoken. Finally, he surrendered and quietly admitted, "I'm called...'Claw' by some."

It was a name he'd not gone by since he was a lad, one his cousin had stuck him with for the creature on his crest, The Dragon. It was a silly name, and for an instant he regretted divulging such a thing to her.

Then he remembered they'd likely die here. She'd never utter the name beyond these walls.


"Claw?"

He grunted in reply.

Hilaire couldn't recall a Sir Claw among her father's men.

Why Claw? Were his fingers malformed? Nay, he'd held her hands in his. They'd felt...perfect.

She wondered what the rest of him looked like. Perhaps if she could see his face, it would set her mind at ease, for his quicksilver temper certainly did nothing to comfort her.

She approached him warily, crouching beside him to help scratch at the dirt. This close, she could detect the faint scent of his bath beneath the tang of leather and sweat, the scent of bergamot and woodruff.

"Do ye...have a family?" she asked.

"Nay." His voice was gruff, short, to the point.

A long silence ensued, broken only by the sound of fingers fruitlessly scraping against earth, a silence Hilaire soon felt compelled to fill.

"Perhaps I've seen ye in my father's ranks. What do ye look like?"

"Plain. Dark. Ye wouldn't remember me."

His abrupt tone irritated her. But she refused to give up. If he wouldn't speak to her, *she* would do the talking.

"Ye're not the knight who rousted de Lancey at the spring tournament?"

"Nay."

She struggled with a cobblestone lodged fast in the dirt. "The Lowlander who plied Lady Anne so diligently with roses last year?"

"Nay."

The stone came loose. She tossed it aside. "Then are ye—"

"Nay! Ye wouldn't know me," he said impatiently. "I'm not your father's knight. I serve no man save the king."

She gasped with new respect. "Ye're a knight-errant."

A fevered flush stole up her cheek.

No man led such a provocative and fascinating life as a knight-errant. She'd sung songs about the wandering swordsmen, and she'd always envied their freedom and independence.

"How thrillin' that must be—pursuin' impossible, noble quests, livin' by your wits and your word, starin' danger in the eyes without flinchin'." She turned impulsively toward him, her cheeks still warm. "But tell me, do ye never get...lonely?"

He stopped at his labors and cleared his throat, as if considering her question. But he answered as briefly as ever. "Nay."

"I think it *must* be lonely bein' a knight-errant," she disagreed. "Perhaps ye have a lady love?" Most of the knights immortalized in song did.

"Nay." He grunted as he plowed his hands hard into the soil, and she worried that he might break his knuckles on a rock.

"Alas, I have no love either," she told him. "Only the wretched beast I'm betrothed to."

Claw made no response, but she heard his labored breathing as he struggled against the unyielding wall.

As they worked in silence, the reality of her situation seeped in to her thoughts like a chill black mist through cracks of a window, surrounding and enveloping her in despair.

She supposed it was pointless to complain about The Dire Dragan, the brute she was to marry, because she wasn't going to get out of here. Even with the aid of a strong knight-errant, they couldn't carve out more than a small burrow in their prison.

They were going to die.

When she thought about dying, she thought about her family and her friends, the flowers that had just begun to pop up in the meadow below her window, the sky and the people and the seasons she would never see again. Soon, despite her determination not to cry, tears wet her lashes, and her heart ached as if it would break in two.

It was a travesty. She was only nineteen summers old. She'd scarcely lived.

She'd never given her favor to a knight in tournament.

Never written a rebus to a secret love on St. Valentine's Day.

Never bestowed her affections upon a man.

Though she battled to stop them, her tears spilled over. Yet even as grief wrapped throttling fingers around her burning throat, angry denial sprouted beneath her sorrow.

It couldn't be true, she decided, desperate for the man with her to speak further reassurances, even if they were untrue.

She couldn't die now.

She was too young, barely a woman.

What reason did fate have to punish her? She'd done nothing so evil.

Except perhaps to run away from her betrothed.

And defy the king.

And leave her entire household in peril.

She swallowed guiltily.

"Can ye play that?" Sir Claw asked quietly. By his gentle demeanor, she wondered if he could sense her despair. If so, he was too chivalrous to mention it.

She blinked back her tears. "The harp?"

He grunted.

"Aye," she said around the ache in her chest. "My father says I play like an angel."

"An angel." He chuckled low. It was a sad sound. "Well, angel, will ye play for me?"

For one instant, her spirits lifted. There was nothing she loved better than playing her harp. What should she play for him? A roundelay to spring? A madrigal about love? A heroic ballad about a knight-errant to inspire him?

Then all at once she remembered her injured hand. Her heart sank.

"I...I can't."

Sir Claw stopped digging. She heard him turn to her.

"My hand was smashed in the rock slide," she explained.

He dropped whatever stone he'd hefted and moved toward her. "Let me see."

His command was absurd. There was nothing to see in the inky black. Nonetheless, she offered him her hand.

She hadn't noticed the pain before, only a cool numbness. In the midst of deadly peril the injury had seemed the least of her worries. Now, as he tenderly cupped the underside of her hand, she grew aware of a deep throbbing ache underlying the sharp sting of torn flesh.

She sucked her breath between her teeth as he carefully examined her fingers one by one. When he tugged on the last one, she gasped in pain.

"'Tis cracked, but I think not broken," he told her. "Have ye a linen underskirt?"

She blinked at his intimate question.

"Ye need a bandage," he explained. "I don't intend to dig our way out o' here only to have ye bleed to death." His words were grim, but his tone was teasing, and she was glad of his gruff care. "If ye'll allow me?"

She withdrew her hand and steeled herself as he crouched before her. His fingertips brushed her bare ankle before they found the hem of her underskirt, sending an enticing warm quiver up her leg. Then he shredded the flimsy fabric, and she winced as the loud ripping split the quiet of the cavern.

His hands upon her wrist felt massive, but far from clumsy. Indeed, he handled her with such tenderness that she wondered if he performed such tasks often. She supposed a knight-errant, traveling alone from tournament to tournament, battle to battle, would have to know how to bandage his own wounds.

He wrapped the linen lightly about her hand, enclosing her cracked finger in a cloth cocoon. He bent his head over her hand while he worked, as if he could perform the task better by at least pretending to see. She shivered as his slow, measured breaths crossed the back of her wrist.

She wondered again what he looked like. He'd said he was dark and plain, but by the breadth of his shoulders, his rugged, masculine voice, and his calming touch, she couldn't imagine him possessing anything less than godlike features.

Where had he come from? His speech was not unlike hers—a melding of English and Scots common along the Borders, where boundaries shifted as often as the tides. Had "Sir Claw" joined her father's forces to secure peace? Or was he simply a mercenary in need of coin?

Hilaire furrowed her brows. Now that she thought about it, he'd never specifically said that he fought for her father. Perhaps he'd only been passing by when the siege...

A strange chill settled upon her shoulders like a blanket of snow. Where exactly *had* the knight come from? There was only one passageway leading from the castle.

"There, lass," he said lightly when he'd finished, "good as new."

"Thank ye." She curled her bandaged hand protectively against her chest, where her heart thumped with foreboding. "Sir Claw?"

"Aye?"

"How is it...that is, how did ye come to be...next to the passageway?"

He stilled, for a moment seemed to vanish, so quiet was he.

She repeated her question. "How did ye come to be...under the wall?" She awaited his answer with bated breath.

He cleared his throat, but her mind raced ahead of his reply.

Of course.

He wasn't one of her father's men.

He'd come from *outside* the castle which could only mean...

Her breath rasped against her ribs, and her words sounded hollow in her ears. "Ye...ye were sappin' the castle, weren't ye?"

His lack of a response damned him.

Betrayal tripped bitterly on her tongue, and her words came out on a thin wisp of breath. "God's blood—ye don't fight for my father at all. Ye fight for *him*. Ye fight for The Dire Dragan."

# CHAPTER 4

ilaire staggered backward, groping behind her with her good hand. She had to get away, get away from him before he...

"Fear not, lass. I—"

"Nay," she warned him, blocking blindly before her with her bandaged hand. "Stay back."

She heard him step toward her, and fright made her throat go dry. Two threats menaced her now—the darkness and her enemy—and she was cornered between them.

"Lass—"

"Get away from me."

"I promise ye—" He took another pace forward.

"Nay!" she cried. Her heart hammered against her ribs as the two evils closed in, one promising to swallow her, the other promising...

"I won't harm ye."

The sharp ledge pricked her back as she retreated to the limits of her prison. "Nay," she hissed, shrinking back against the wall like a snake ready to strike.

"Don't be afraid," he assured her, continuing his stealthy advance.

All at once, he grabbed her wrist.

She gasped, struggling wildly in his steely grip.

"Lass," he said, tightening his hold, "trust me."

"Let me go," she breathed, twisting her fingers and trying to press him away with her free forearm.

"I can't do that."

"Then leave me here," she bargained. Fear pitched her voice high, and she raced over the words. "Go on without me. Tell him I've died. I'll pay ye. I'll pay ye well."

"I made ye a vow."

"Aye, ye vowed to see me safe." Lord, he was strong as a bull. Why could she not pry free? "Yet ye'll hand me over to him. Ye'll give me to The Dire Dragan."

"Lass, I gave ye my word—"

"The word of an enemy?" Her voice was brittle.

"My word as a knight. I vow I will not force ye to anythin' against your will."

"But ye're sworn to *him*. Ye're beholden to that...that beast!"

He released her so abruptly she nearly tumbled backward. She heard his deep sigh as he stepped away from her.

She was free. He'd let her go. She waited for a wave of relief to wash over her.

It never came. He'd loosed her, aye, but she still languished in the dark, trapped and terrified. And now she'd alienated her sole source of comfort. She'd doused her only light against the darkness.

Catching her breath, she wrapped her arms about her. Empty and cool, they were little consolation. She sought and found her harp and hugged it fiercely. But it, too, gave her no ease. And as she tried in vain to re-create the comfort Sir Claw had offered her, the shadows of the night crept closer and closer.

He didn't seem to notice them. He'd begun to grapple again with the wall, gouging away steadily. But she felt their presence—tangible, menacing. She felt the weight of them, pressing in on her, feeding on her fear. Her heart fluttered, and her breathing grew shallow.

As the dark wraiths advanced with their ebony cloaks to smother her, Sir Claw's digging grew distant, muffled, until the sound echoed curiously like the scratching of a rat in a hollow log. The edges of reality blurred into watery waves of black, then disappeared altogether.

She'd fainted. Or died. She wasn't certain which.

When she returned to awareness, the world was tipped askew. She lay flat on her back. Swirls of gray and silver, coal and pewter danced on an ethereal current before her eyes.

"Lass!" His whisper was urgent, anxious.

She groaned as a fierce throbbing in her head suddenly commanded her attention. Nay, she wasn't dead. Unless this was the punishment of hell.

He smacked her cheeks lightly, clapping her face with his rough palms until annoyance shredded the last of the silvery cobwebs from her eyes and she dizzily sat up.

"Are ye all right?" he asked, his voice tense.

"I will be if ye'll cease beatin' me," she bit out.

Her complaint evidently spurred great relief in him, for he let out a shuddering sigh that seemed to come from the depths of his being.

"I feared…" he began.

She waited, breathless. She knew what he feared. He'd feared she was dead. She prayed he wouldn't say it.

"I feared ye'd steal all the air with your snorin'," he said. His words, so unexpected, so knavish, took a moment to register.

"Snorin'!" she cried. "I don't…"

She shoved in his general direction and successfully toppled him. But the sweetness of her triumph was nothing compared to the sweetness of his laughter reverberating in the cave. It was a low rumble, deep and rich, like well-ripened mead. And though he offered only a sip of it, she curiously longed to taste more.

She had to remind herself that he was the enemy. Sir Claw would surely turn her over to The Dire Dragan as soon as they were free.

If they ever got free.

She swallowed at the sobering thought.

Yet, until they escaped, they were jailed in this prison together, helpless, fighting for the same liberty. For the moment he seemed civil enough. He wouldn't harm her. He had no cause to harm her. At least not yet.

And, she realized with a sudden trip of her heart, Sir Claw was not unpleasant, for a foe. Actually, he was rather congenial, warm, and chivalrous...except for that remark about her snoring. And even that brought a smile to her lips. The man was obviously no lack-wit.

Aye, she thought, Sir Claw had given her comfort and brought a twinkle to her eye. He hadn't mocked her for weeping or fainting, but had gallantly offered her what comfort he could.

How could she despise him?

She could not. They were allies waging a war against a common enemy. So she'd fight beside him.

Giric was shaking like a newborn pup. It was absurd. Aye, for one terrible moment, he'd thought Hilaire was dead. The dull thud as she hit the ground and her awful stillness when he flung himself to her side had driven his heart up into his throat, where it seemed to lodge until he heard her breathe again.

But they were dying anyway. What did it matter if she fainted now? Sleep might spare her the unbearable thirst and lethal lethargy surely to come.

Yet what he'd almost said to her, what he'd almost admitted aloud was not that he'd feared she was dead.

It was that he feared she'd *left him.*

As hardened as he should be to his own curse, to his own failings, he couldn't bear to lose another woman. Damn the Fates—if he did nothing else before he died, he'd at least redeem his soul by fulfilling this final vow. If it wracked his body and broke his spirit, he would see her out of this hell.

With renewed vigor, he attacked the wall, pounding and scraping as if demons chased him. To his astonishment, in a moment Hilaire joined the battle, fighting aggressively beside him. Soon the sounds of their frayed breathing filled the cave, punctuated by blows of rock on rock and grunts of exertion.

They might have gone on silently, wrapped up in their own thoughts, digging away until they either broke through to freedom or ran out of air. But an overwhelming need to enlighten Hilaire gnawed at Giric like a rat. For pride or honor, he simply couldn't let her believe what she believed about her betrothed.

"He's not a beast," he murmured between blows, before he had the chance to think better of it.

"What?" she said, panting. "What did ye say?"

"The Dragan." He continued to dig. "He's only a man. He wouldn't harm ye."

She sniffed. "He drowned his first wife and child."

The image came to him unbidden—his darling Mary and their four-year-old daughter, Katie, frolicking upon the daisy-strewn lap of a May meadow. Katie had been the light of his life, Mary the first woman he'd ever loved. And the last.

That year, the river had run high, swollen by spring rains till it swept and whirled toward the sea with delirious speed. The grasses and trees had grown green and lush on the bounty.

Wee Katie had called him a big black bear. He'd growled and stomped after the giggling pair—his wife and his daughter—and they'd dashed off to hide among the thick hedge and saplings along the river's edge.

That had been his last happy memory with them.

In the next painful moments, the two of them, his precious ladies, simply disappeared.

A crofter found them hours later, pulled them from the river. By then their faces were as pale and lifeless as linen. Their long hair, bedecked with bits of twigs and leaves and weeds, was wrapped around their drenched bodies like fishing net.

Giric's voice grew husky with the memory. "They were drowned. But not by his hand. 'Twas an accident. He tried to save them. He did everything he could to..." To his horror, a wretched sob stuck in his throat. He swallowed it down like tough venison. "He tried to save them."

Hilaire made no reply. He wondered if she believed him. He wondered if he believed himself.

He'd gone over the events a thousand times in his head. He'd chided himself for chasing them that day, for letting them out of his sight, even for allowing them out of doors. He'd searched wildly for them afterward, diving into the icy water time and time again, bellowing their names till his voice grew hoarse and he could call them no longer.

Yet he was still racked with the harrowing obsession that he could have done more.

"Ye seem to know The Dragan well," she said quietly.

"Nay. I've only heard what others say, those who knew him...before."

"Before?"

He thought of the lad he'd once been, and an ache filled his throat, like the profound longing for a departed loved one. He'd been happy once, full of life, eager and ambitious and brimming with young dreams. He'd made men laugh and maidens sigh. Now he only inspired fear.

"Before...he was cursed," he grumbled.

He wrenched a stone from its earthen bed. There was no point in dwelling on the past, on dreams that were long dead.


Hilaire bit her lip. Somehow she'd offended Sir Claw. She could tell by the violence with which he tossed bits of stone aside. He obviously didn't wish to talk ill of his overlord. He clearly bore some loyalty for his beastly master. Perhaps he was irritated with her for threatening to break her betrothal. Or perhaps he was only angry with her for talking when she should be digging.

She frowned. She was doing her best, considering the wall was as hard as marble and she could only dig with one hand. As for squirming out of marriage, she supposed it was not very worthy of her. But contrary to what Sir Claw believed, there must be a kernel of truth in the gruesome tales about The Dire Dragan, and she had no intention of discovering it at her own peril.

So she redoubled her efforts, using a pointed rock to chip away at the soil. And she kept quiet, neither wishing to disturb her rescuer nor draw undue attention to her own shortcomings.

They worked side by side for what seemed like an hour, the only sounds their driven breathing, the dull thud of rock on earth, and the low rustle of his chainmail.

Earlier she'd shivered in the passageway. Now she was drenched in sweat. Salty drops rolled down her brow and stung her eyes, and her bandaged hand throbbed in pain.

The air felt thick, and yet it was hard to draw enough of it into her lungs. She wondered what it felt like to suffocate. She was frightened. She didn't want to die.

Tears brimmed in her eyes again. She refused to shed them. After all, the man already considered her a coward for running from her betrothed. She'd be damned if she'd let him believe she was a spineless, weeping milksop.

"Ye need to rest," he said, startling her.

"Nay, I'll be..." Her voice caught.

He wrapped his fingers around her forearm and gently pulled her away from the wall.

"Ye need to rest," he repeated. "Besides, 'twill save the air."

She squeezed her eyes shut tightly. It was as she feared. Already they were running out of air. Already they were dying. She reined in her panic only by force of sheer will. And still a great sobbing gasp escaped her.

Suddenly both of her arms were clasped in his hands, and she could feel the weight of his blind gaze upon her.

"I'm sorry," she whispered, cursing her rogue tears.

He bit out a quiet oath. Then to her astonishment, his hand crooked around the back of her neck, and he pulled her to his chest. The manly scent of him filled her nose as he held her against his hauberk. Yet his arms—his enemy arms—lent her strange comfort.

He wasted no breath in chiding her, nor did he ply her with words of solace. He only held her, stroking her hair with one hand while she buried her sobs against his wide chest.

She should have felt shame, she supposed, blubbering her salty tears all over the poor man's armor. Yet he gallantly made no mention of it.

Indeed, she felt so calmed by his embrace—the strength of his body, the gentleness of his hand, the warmth of his ragged breath upon her face—that she forgot for a short while that he was her foe.

Giric felt the stone rampart surrounding his heart shudder as the lass nestled closer to him.

As if she relied upon him.

As if she belonged there.

What had made him reach for her, he didn't know. It was no concern of his if she wept. She'd likely weep a loch's worth of tears before the ordeal was over.

Yet taking her in his arms had seemed the right thing to do.

Now he was certain it was a mistake. She brought back too many memories, too much pain. Her soft sobbing snagged at his heart. The sweet scent of her hair insinuated its way into his soul. And the feel of her body against his—warm, innocent, trusting—was almost more than he could bear.

How long had it been since someone—anyone—had given him such trust, such belief?

Oh aye, his men believed in him. They believed The Dire Dragan was a fierce and fearless warrior. They wagered daily on that belief with their lives.

But no one had trusted *him,* Giric, for a long time.

*Nor should they,* he thought bitterly. No woman should welcome his cursed embrace, and if Hilaire knew what was good for her...

Yet she felt so perfect in his arms. For one greedy instant he closed his eyes and imagined she was his, all of her—her silken tresses, her soft voice, her pliant body. The sweet vision nearly crumbled the bastion of his heart.

And then he let her go.

If by chance her soft moan was one of protest, he didn't wish to know. He set her gently aside.

"Tell me..." he croaked, barely able to speak across the empty space her sudden absence created. "Tell me about your family." If he kept her talking, she'd be less likely to dwell on the troubles at hand. And perhaps her chatter would distract him from his own foolish imaginings.

"My family?" Her whisper was rough, groggy, as if she'd just awakened. He didn't want to think of the sensual image it conjured.

"Aye," he said, turning again to delve at the wall and trying to lighten his tone as he spoke over his shoulder. "What is your father like when he's not a commander o' men?"

"He is a good man," she said, "honest and fair. Just, but very firm."

"Ah. But I'd wager ye have him suppin' from your fingers."

"Sometimes." Her low giggle surprised him. "How could ye tell?"

"I had a daughter once."

"Ye said ye had no family."

"She...died, along with her mother."

She gave a wee gasp. "How awful for ye."

"'Twas a long time ago." Not long enough to erase the pain in his voice.

"I lost my mother when I was a child," she told him. "She fell ill. I remember listenin' to her, night after night, coughin' and coughin'. 'Twas a horrible sound."

Giric remembered that sound. Four years had passed, but he could still recall his second wife's wheezing breaths as she struggled to find air in the fluid drowning her. "But not so horrible as the night it ceased."

"Aye. I blamed myself. For years afterward I thought I'd caused her death by prayin' she'd stop coughin'."

Her words struck a familiar and dissonant chord in him. He, too, had prayed for an end to Elaine's suffering.

"Did ye ever blame yourself for her death?" Hilaire asked, startling him with her candor.

"Nay," he lied. "The physicians did all they could—bled her, gave her poultices to draw out the sickness." He blew out a tired breath. "I even summoned a healer the chaplain claimed was a handmaiden o' the devil."

"Ye must have loved her well," Hilaire whispered.

"I...cared for her." He hadn't dared to love Elaine, not after losing his first wife. She'd simply been the king's choice, a political alliance. Though he'd treated her with respect, he'd stubbornly closed his heart to her.

Until she'd taken ill. Then, forced to watch her face an agonizing death with courage—her sweetness unwavering, her faith undimmed—he grew to care for her deeply. Which was the cruelest blow of all. For when she finally succumbed, it was as if a piece of him had been torn away.

Worse, while he knelt, stunned with grief, beside her fresh grave, vicious tongues began to wag. And before long, the rumor grew legs.

The Dire Dragan had struck once more. He must have poisoned his wife.

"Have ye never loved again?" Hilaire's voice broke into his thoughts.

"Nay." This time he didn't lie. After losing two wives and a daughter, he'd kept his heart under lock and key. To his third wife, he'd shown courtesy and companionship, no more.

"What o' your parents?" she asked.

"Dead." It was no great loss in his mind. His father had been a cruel and ill-tempered Highlander, killed in a clan brawl he'd probably instigated. His mother had been feeble, living at the mercy of her husband's fists most of her life.

"I'm sorry," she said.

"That, too, happened long ago."

"Indeed? How old *are* ye?" Hilaire asked.

He smiled humorlessly. "Old as Methuselah." He felt that old at least, despite the fact he was in the prime of his life. "I've just passed my twenty-sixth year."

She laughed, and he thought how incongruous the sound was in this tomb. "As old as that? And just what have ye done to pass all o' this tedious eternity then, Sir Claw?"

Giric furrowed his brow in puzzlement. Was the lass flirting with him? It had been so long since he'd heard the lilting music of a woman's jesting that he hardly recognized it. But aye, it seemed she curved her words around a coy smile.

So how could he answer her? He'd done nothing but eat, breathe, fight, and mourn for years. But there was a time…

"I suppose ye haven't much time for pleasure," she said, filling in the silence, as he found most women were wont to do, this one in particular, "what with travelin' from place to place, goin' on noble quests and so forth."

He raised a brow, a gesture completely wasted in the darkness. The only noble quest he'd ever undertaken was trying to catch a butterfly for his wee Katie.

"And how have *ye* filled the hours?" he asked her.

"With music." He could feel her passion for it like a living thing in the dark.

"The harp."

"Aye."

Before she could be reminded of her injury again, he intervened. "When we are out o' here then, lass, and ye're fully healed, will ye favor me with a performance?"

"Aye," she softly replied.

"I count upon it." His lip curved up into a wry smile. "Perhaps ye shall sing o' the great underworld adventures o' Sir Claw and Lady Hilaire."

"Aye, and ye'll accompany me on the rock wall."

Her gurgle of laughter washed over him like a healing balm. He couldn't help but wonder what kind of joy he might have found listening to a lifetime of that delightful sound.

# CHAPTER 5

There was little enough air in their prison, certainly not enough for idle chatter. But Giric took pleasure in the sound of Hilaire's voice, and she reveled in conversation. Exchanging pleasantries seemed the best way to keep her demons at bay. So he obliged her as he chafed away at the wall, though he doubted he'd uttered as many words in a month of days before now.

"Tell me o' your adventures, if we're to immortalize them in song," she entreated playfully, reminding him of his daughter asking for stories by the evening hearth. "What great feats o' prowess have ye undertaken? What dragons have ye slain?"

"No dragons," he said, chuckling. "Dragonflies perhaps."

"Have ye saved a maiden in distress before?"

"Maiden in distress." He paused to think. "Once I rescued a damsel from a swarm o' bees."

"And how did ye do that? Did ye battle them with your sword? Lay siege to their hive? Gallantly let them sting ye while she escaped?"

He grinned at the memory. Though it had worked brilliantly, Elaine had been none too grateful for his rescue. "I tossed her into the moat."

"Oh, Sir Claw, ye didn't!"

He rather liked the sound of that silly name on her lips. And he liked the way she chided him.

"What about ye?" he asked. "Any feats o' great renown?"

She sighed. "Alas, nay. I am my father's youngest, his only lass, and he guards me like a mastiff. My brothers have seen the world," she said enviously, "but I've ne'er set foot outside my home."

"Ne'er?" Giric asked, incredulous. A wealth of images suddenly riffled through his mind like pages of a book—scenes of the stark Syrian desert and the steamy Tunisian coast, of crumbling Roman temples and lush Greek olive groves, Flemish towns crowded with craftsmen and fishmongers, and Paris, where velvet-clad nobles encrusted with jewels shared the streets with waifs and rats. To take her there, to see it all again through her unworldly eyes...

But it would never be. She feared The Dire Dragan. Even if, by some incredible quirk of fate, they got out alive, it would be on another man's arm she'd discover the world, for he intended to keep his promise to her, to grant her her freedom.

"I wager ye've traveled far and wide," she marveled.

"Some."

"Tell me about all the places ye've seen." He could almost hear the sparkle in her eyes.

He paused to lean against the rock wall and think. "My father took me to Spain when I was four." Odd, but he hadn't thought of that journey in years. "'Twas the first time I'd seen the sea." He smiled. "I waded in the waves near the dock, and he chided me for ruinin' my new boots."

"Is it as vast as they say?"

"What—Spain?"

"The sea."

He blinked. "Ye've never seen..." Sweet Mary—she *was* sheltered. He wiped the sweat from his careworn brow with the back of his hand. He'd always loved the sea, but how could one describe it? "'Tis magnificent. The water stretches as far as ye can see, like an enormous coverlet, till it meets the edge o' the sky. Its hue is always changin'—blue, green, silver—and sometimes the wind whips the peaks o' the waves to white froth. Ye can taste salt in the breeze, and when ye're far from shore, the only sounds ye hear are the lappin' o' waves against the ship, the creak o' the hull, the slap o' the sails, the screech o' the gulls circlin' above the open water."

"The open water," she sighed. "I should like to sail on a ship."

And he should like to take her, to share the ecstasy of wild ocean breezes caressing their arms, salt spray bedewing their faces, to point out the sleek silver dolphins that followed the vessel, leaping and frolicking and chattering like playful children.

"Tell me more about your travels," she demanded, her appetite whetted.

He should be tunneling at the wall. Time was slipping away, and their discourse wasted precious air. But it had been so long since he'd engaged in agreeable patter with such a charming companion. Her words were like sweet mulled claret to his parched spirit.

"I was born in the Highlands, in Glen Coe."

"Glen Coe," she repeated reverently.

"The country is rugged there. The mountains weep with waterfalls. In the fall, the heather turns, and 'tis like the hills wear a plaid o' purple and gold."

"Oh," she breathed. Then she hungrily asked, "And then where?"

"I earned my spurs in the Lowlands, at Rivenloch."

"Indeed? What was your first battle?"

"I fought in the Holy Land."

"On Crusade?"

"Aye." Those images were not so joyous. But despite grim memories of poverty and bloodshed, he recalled other things—the warmth of the desert wind, the magnificence of the walled cities.

"What was it like?"

"The fightin' was ugly. But the country... The air is scented everywhere with exotic spices—myrrh and cinnamon and frankincense," he remembered, "and the ladies wear layers o' cloth as sheer as mist and in every color o' the rainbow."

"Was...*he*...with ye then? The Dire Dragan?"

Her question caught him off guard. "Nay. I...came after the death o' his first wife." In a sense, it was true. Giric mac Leod—the man he once was—had been buried by The Dire Dragan, sunk into the grave beside his wife and daughter.

"Were ye not afraid o' him, o' his curse?"

Aye, Giric thought, that curse was the *only* thing he feared. Instead he said, "I've ne'er judged a man by the misfortune that plagues him."

"Some say 'tis more than misfortune. Some say he's," she murmured, ending in a whisper, "the servant o' Lucifer."

"God's eyes." Giric didn't mean to swear, but it was just such gossip that had made his life a living hell. Just because he'd lost faith in a god who would tear away all the beauty in his life didn't mean he was the devil's minion. "The Dire Dragan is a man, no more, no less, and anyone who—"

Her hand made awkward contact with his chest. "Fie! 'Twas wicked o' me, speakin' thus o' your lord. Forgive me."

It wasn't her words, but rather her proximity, her warm breath upon his cheek, and the womanly scent of her, that instantly cooled his wrath. He wanted to take her in his arms again, to feel the slender nape of her neck and the playful caress of her hair. Forgive her? He wanted to embrace her.

But when he didn't respond, she withdrew her hand.

"To be fair," he sighed with a twinge of disappointment, "ye say nothin' that hasn't been voiced a thousand times."

"But ye clearly care for him to leap so quickly to his defense. He must count himself fortunate to have such a loyal vassal."

Giric didn't know how to answer her.

She didn't seem to require an answer. "Tell me, what is it about him ye admire?"

He puzzled over the question. Was there anything left of Giric mac Leod in The Dire Dragan? Anything he could be proud of?

He supposed his stoic suffering counted for something.

And there was still his sense of justice.

He was generally a man of peace, preferring diplomacy to the sword.

And he was unflinchingly loyal to the king.

But Hilaire probably wouldn't understand any of that. She believed in shining knights who saved damsels from dragons.

Quietly, she added, "Tell me why a woman should desire to marry him."

His heart skipped a beat.

Was Hilaire reconsidering her escape?

Was she asking him to persuade her to honor the betrothal?

He couldn't do that. Not in good conscience. He might convince her that The Dire Dragan was not an ogre, that he was undeserving of the taunts that dogged him. Indeed, he longed to purge that poison from his soul.

But nothing would lift the curse destiny had placed upon his wretched name.

"He is...fair," he decided, "in trade and in battle."

She muttered low, "Yet he storms my father's keep."

"Only to claim what is his by rights."

She mulled that over and couldn't seem to come up with a defense. "What else? How else is he worthy?"

He thought for a moment. "He works hard. He trains hard. He's generous with his hospitality. He's frugal with his coin."

He smirked. Upon reflection, that last might not seem a virtue to the lass. Mary and Katie had begged him endlessly to spend his coin on ribbons or cloth dolls or a jeweled trinket every time a peddler came to the gate.

"Does he play music?" Was that hope he heard in her voice?

"Nay."

"Oh." She sounded discouraged.

He added quickly, "But he likes to hear it. At least he used to."

"Ye mean, before he started ki—, before his wives were killed?"

Giric bristled. She still doubted him. Pointedly, he told her, "Aye, before his wife and daughter fell in the river and were drowned."

"Mm. But his second wife, she was poisoned, aye?"

"She died from sickness," he said wearily.

"Sickness? Like *your* wife?"

"What?"

"Like *your* wife. Ye said your wife died o' sickness."

"Oh, aye."

"And what about his last wife, the one they say he beat?"

His blood began to simmer. He bit out a reply between his teeth. "He'd sooner cut off his arm than lift it against a woman."

"But he pushed her from a tower and—"

"Nay!" he shouted, startling even himself with the vehemence of his denial. After that, against his better judgment and against his will, his thoughts poured from him like ale from a cracked barrel, and there was nothing he could do to stop them. "He would ne'er do such a thing. She flung *herself* from that tower. He had no part in it."

Even now, Giric wondered at the veracity of his words. Was he truly blameless? Could he have stopped her? Could he have reached her in time?

"Why would she do that?" Hilaire pressed.

He blew out a quick breath. "She was afraid...very, very afraid."

"O' him?"

"O' herself." He swallowed hard. He'd never spoken to anyone about the horrible agonies Bess had endured.

"Herself?"

He rested his head back against the rock wall. He'd wanted to talk about it for months now. He'd longed to tell someone what had truly happened.

But he'd been afraid. Afraid no one would believe him. Then afraid they *would* believe him. And if they did, they might dig up poor Bess's body and bury her in unhallowed ground.

Here in the dark, staring death in the face, he could finally say what he wished. There was no one to judge him, no one to tell him that he was a devil or that Bess was a witch.

He let out a shuddering sigh. When he spoke, his words were as quiet as thoughts.

"It started as voices she heard whisperin' in her head, tellin' her evil things. She tried to ignore them. But they wouldn't go away. Before long, she began speakin' to them. Yellin' at them. Cursin'."

That had been the most painful, listening to gentle Bess shriek at imaginary demons in a voice that no longer belonged to her.

"Still they haunted her," he continued. "Soon she began seein' them. She imagined they were attackin' her. She'd beat herself purple with a poker, tryin' to pry their claws free. Her arms were slashed with cuts from her own dagger and, when I took that from her, her fingernails. She shunned her clothin', claimin' the demons would only steal it from her. And oft she wandered naked through the halls o' the keep. In her madness, she tore out her hair and lit her veil on fire." He swallowed hard at the memory. "Then one fateful night, her mind cleared long enough for her to see what had happened to her, how mad she'd become. She couldn't bear to live with the torment any longer. Before I... Before anyone could stop her, she leaped from the tower ledge...and broke on the stones below."

Hilaire could scarcely breathe. The story was horrifying. But it wasn't the story that paralyzed her. It was his telling of it.

*I,* Sir Claw had said. *I* took the dagger from her.

The truth was almost too amazing to believe, but there could be no other explanation. Sir Claw must be The Dire Dragan.

Giric was the given name of her betrothed, not Claw, but no matter what he called himself, he was The Dire Dragan. His slip of the tongue had betrayed him.

And yet, she might have uncovered his secret anyway, for who but a loved one could speak so intimately of a woman's mind? Who else would know her so well? The ragged timbre of pain in his voice described not the distant suffering of a witness, but the agony of a husband.

This was him. Sir Claw was The Dire Dragan.

A frisson of cold panic raced along her spine. She was trapped with him. Alone. In the dark.

He knew who she was. And he knew she abhorred him.

God's eyes—what would he do to her?

He *was* cursed. It was certain now. They'd not yet exchanged the vows of marriage, yet already he brought her death.

Her heart stuttered, and she felt the walls closing in again. But before she raced into headlong anxiety, he spoke.

"Forgive me. 'Twas not my intent to upset ye."

The words stuck in her dry throat. "'Tis...'tis...it must have been dreadful for y-your lord."

He grunted in agreement. "He's had a lifetime o' sorrow."

That was all he said. But he spoke simply and from the heart.

*He's had a lifetime o' sorrow.*

While the words hung in the air—raw, naked, vulnerable—suddenly their truth rang out like a hollow bell in the melancholy dark, dispelling all of Hilaire's doubts.

The Dire Dragan was no ogre. He was but a man, a sad and lonely man. Adversity had dropped a heavy burden upon him, a burden he clearly didn't deserve. Fate had been unkind to him. He'd suffered terrible tragedies, unspeakable losses. But that didn't mean he was forever cursed. And it didn't mean he was a monster.

Her heart melted, and she yearned to console him, this lost soul with the broken spirit.

"Perhaps," she allowed, "I've been too hasty in my judgment. Perhaps he's not cursed so much as—"

"Nay, ye have it right," he snapped. "He *is* cursed. But by fate, not by his own deeds."

She could hear it now—the bitterness, the anguish—hidden appreciably by his gruff voice, but nonetheless there.

"Well, then," she murmured in all humility, "as ye say, I should not judge him by his misfortune."

A weighty silence ensued. If she hoped he'd reveal himself now, she was disappointed.

Instead, he returned to his labors.

She, too, scraped at the wall, but her mind flitted about so wildly she scarcely heeded her own progress.

After a long while, he rested, and his weary panting filled the cave.

"Pity 'tis a harp ye play and not a clarion," he said in a rare moment of wry humor. "Otherwise, we could fell the walls as Joshua did."

She grinned at his unexpected wit, which threw her into an even more complex melee of thoughts.

Who was he truly? Who was The Dire Dragan? All she knew of him was what she'd heard, largely improbable tales about his vicious nature, his dark moods, and the curse that followed him. Certainly this was not the man with her now.

This man spoke kindly, nobly. He'd offered her comfort. He'd dug his way to her when she cried out for help. He'd breathed with her, bandaged her injured hand. He'd held her when her fears got the best of her and anxiously seen to her when she'd fainted. He'd promised to get her out, even knowing she thought him a monster, even knowing...

They were unlikely to escape.

She tried to swallow the knot of dread choking her, but it lodged like a gallows noose against her throat.

He knew they were doomed. He knew, because he was cursed. The pall of misery hung over him. All his wives had died tragically. She was destined to be another victim of The Dire Dragan.

Yet he'd hidden it from her. Why?

Because she was frightened, and he didn't wish to frighten her more. It was no matter to him that she'd tried to flee their marriage, that she'd said awful, hurtful things about him, that she'd poked and prodded at his painful history as if it were fiction lived by some hapless character in a fable. Still he protected her. Still he did all in his power to save her.

She had sadly misjudged the man who was to have been her husband. And now, because of her cowardly flight, she had doomed the both of them. She wished she could turn back time's plow and unfurrow the ruts she'd gouged in their lives. But it was too late.

Lord Giric resumed working with scarcely a moment's repose, toiling away at his Herculean task with no complaint.

She ought to let him stop. It was clear he only dug at the wall to stave off her despair. He'd been right at the beginning. There was no escaping this grievous tomb.

She bit her lip to quell its trembling. She refused to panic. The Dire Dragan, Giric, had carried a heavy enough burden in his life for three men. She wouldn't add herself to the weight he bore. She'd suffer in silence. And if she could do anything to ease his spirit, say anything to make amends for the harsh words she'd spoken...

A trickle of tiny stones rattled along the wall to Hilaire's right. It was an innocent sound, and yet it prickled the tiny hairs along the back of her neck.

"What was—" she began.

"Hist!"

Tense as the highest string on her harp, Hilaire waited, her ears pricked up for the slightest noise. But none followed.

After a long moment, Giric turned back to the wall. "Must have been a—"

Before he could finish his sentence, a deep growl like thunder shook the ground. Suddenly Hilaire relived the nightmare of the rockslide all over again.

Rocks rumbled and pounded and shrieked. Giric gave her a forceful shove that drove her to her knees, out of the way. Still, metallic dust tainted the air, smothering her, and a barrage of cobbles battered her arms as she crossed them protectively over her head.

This time, in a few moments, it was over. And, miraculously, she was mostly unhurt. She gagged on mildewy dust and coughed it free of her lungs, flaring her nostrils to seek breathable air.

Perhaps, she dared to hope, groping about her, the stones had shifted in their favor.

Perhaps the passageway was clear now.

Perhaps his sapping tunnel had been reopened.

"Can ye...see anythin'?" she asked, unable to conceal the excitement in her voice. "Can ye see light?" She patted the rocks around her and ventured forth at a crouch.

"Sir Claw?"

The taste of metal grew suddenly strong in her mouth.

"Sir Claw?"

It was the taste of fear.

She scrabbled about more urgently now, running even her injured hand along the uneven ground.

"Sir..."

Her fingers contacted chainmail, then the buckle of a greave behind his knee, and she sighed in relief.

He was here. He was still here. After pushing her out of the way to protect her from the collapse, he must have dived for the ground. Perhaps he was too stunned to move.

"Sir Claw, I was so worried. Are ye..."

Her fingers shrunk atop his mailed calf.

"Giric?"

There was no reply, no movement. Her heart thrumming furiously, she traced her fingers up along the back of his leg, past the poleyn to his thigh. But there she was forced to stop.

An enormous boulder straddled his motionless body, pinning him to the ground, crushing him like grain beneath a millstone.

# CHAPTER 6

"Nay," she breathed. "Nay!"

She tugged hard on his leg, terrified, desperate, but he didn't respond. The word rasped from her over and over like a metal file on an iron pot, scraping her throat.

"Nay!"

He couldn't be dead. She'd just been talking to him. He wouldn't have left her. Not when she needed him. Sweet Saints—she couldn't bear to die alone. Horror seeped out of her on that one piercing syllable.

"Nay!"

Her own labored breathing grated on her ears, and she knew it would turn to whimpers if she didn't seize command of her wits. This was no time to indulge in selfish panic.

Despite her fears, there was a chance Giric was still alive. And if so, Hilaire was his only hope. With a determined shake of her head, she clenched her fists and gradually willed her terror to subside.

When she'd regained a modicum of control, she set about examining him more thoroughly. She could feel nothing through his chainmail leggings except thick muscle. But she discovered if she lay flat against the tunnel floor, she could slip her good arm into the crevice beneath the boulder, along the length of him, and find his hand.

As she clasped his limp fingers, tears started in her eyes. His knuckles were raw. She could feel the jagged edges of broken fingernails. His hand was slippery with blood, not from the avalanche, but from the pointless digging he had done for her sake.

Then, as she traced questing fingers over the pads of his callused hand, she found a miracle. A pulse beat in his wrist. He was yet alive.

A wordless cry of joy escaped her, unfettered for a brief moment by the fact that her situation was no less hopeless.

He was still trapped beneath the boulder.

They were still imprisoned within the earth.

And the shadows still pressed in upon her.

Reluctantly, she let go of his hand and knelt by the boulder. She clasped her fingers before her and squeezed her eyes tightly shut in prayer.

"Dear God, please forgive your wayward servant her trespasses." She blushed to think how many trespasses stained her soul, considering how much trouble she'd caused. "I have sinned much against this man who was to be my husband. But I beseech ye, do not take him to your bosom, not yet." She shifted, and a sharp rock bit into the bare skin of her knee, but she tolerated it like a penitent monk enduring the lash. "He is a good man, a kind man, and I have done him much wrong. But if ye will save him, if ye will deliver him from death's arms…"

She opened her eyes, nonplussed. What? What would she promise? What could she bargain with?

She gulped.

He *was* a good man. He was a *wonderful* man. Aye, he'd had his share of misfortune, and there was an air of gloom about him. But wasn't it her maid Martha who was always saying the love of a good woman could transform a man from a beast to a prince?

She raised her chin and made up her mind.

"If ye let him live, God, I vow…I vow I will willingly marry The Dire Dragan." Her voice shook under the weight of her promise. "I will care for him and honor him and bear him babes."

For a moment, she felt dizzy. What was she promising? She hadn't even seen his face. She didn't truly know him. And yet she supposed she knew him better than many brides knew their husbands-to-be.

"I will love him as a wife must love her husband…for as long as I shall live."

She couldn't help but wonder how long that would be, considering his curse. Nonetheless, she made the sign of the cross and rocked back on her heels.

Then she waited.

No light suddenly appeared before her.

No sound disturbed the silence.

No miraculous burst of lightning or crack of thunder parted the rock to set them free.

She reached her hand out for Giric's calf and gave it a jiggle, but he didn't respond.

Now she grew vexed.

Satan's ballocks—she'd just promised away the most valuable thing she had to offer.

What more could God want? Did he not hear her plea? Did he not understand her sacrifice?

Or perhaps, she thought, lifting her chin against the painful insult, God considered her beyond redemption.

A tear squeezed out between her lashes, but she angrily swiped it from her cheek.

She would show him. She would show God. If he wouldn't help her, she'd do it without him. She'd bring Giric mac Leod back to the living, even if she had to wrestle the devil to do it herself.

Pushing up her sleeves, she started jostling the dozing knight wholeheartedly.

"Wake up! Wake up, damn ye! We're never goin' to get out o' here if ye don't wake up. Do ye hear me?"

She poked at his calf.

"I know who ye are. But know this: I'm not afraid o' ye. And I don't believe in your damned curse."

She shook his leg like a mastiff shaking a rabbit.

"Wake up, ye…ye selfish knave! What kind o' knight are ye to desert a lady in her hour o' need?"

She raised her fist and pummeled the back of his leg until her knuckles were scraped from the chainmail and tears rolled down her face.

"Wake up, Dragan! Wake up, ye son of a harlot! Wake…"

It was no use. His heart might beat, but he was as dead to her as wood.

She slumped onto her hindquarters, defeated. Her hand struck the low strings of her harp, which had somehow survived the rockslide, and out of habit, she gathered the instrument to her bosom.

No sooner had she surrendered to despair than the shadows of her mind began to creep in. They'd been there all along, she realized.

Waiting for her.

Waiting while she played her silly little game.

Waiting for her to succumb to their embrace.

She felt them coming for her, promising peace, delivering death. She shuddered and clung to the harp like a magic amulet.

"Ye're not real," she murmured, but her voice was weak and uncertain.

The shadows answered her, pressing closer, brushing their chill fingers atop her shoulder, against

her cheek, over her eyes. She gasped and felt a cold rush of air enter her lungs, as if one of them had dived down her throat to claim her from the inside. She closed her lips against a scream and dug her fingers into her harp, engraving the wood with crescents from her nails.

She had to think of something else, anything but the ominous shapes surrounding her.

Her music.

Her maidservant.

The flowers outside her window.

The sea.

The sea...

Giric had told her about the sea.

She closed her eyes and imagined it lay before her—an enormous coverlet stretching as far as the horizon, the fabric shifting from gray to green to blue, white frothy caps bobbing up toward the vast sky—the vast, open, bright, cloudless sky.

She saw it clearly now. The sun sparkled on the waves. Seabirds circled overhead. And she stood on the desk of a grand ship, slicing through the sea like shears through silk. She took a long, deep breath, and she swore she could almost taste the crisp brine air.

They were gone now. The shadows were gone, fled to the corners, vanquished by the vision Giric had given her.

Giric.

She had to save him. Somehow she had to get him from beneath that boulder.

She set her harp aside and groped her way toward his legs again. She crouched, seized his ankles, and tugged backward, wincing as needles of pain shot through her injured hand. The gravel skidded beneath her heels, but his body didn't budge. He was imprisoned by the rock.

Gingerly, aware she was touching him in a most inappropriate manner, she ran her hand up along the back of his thigh and over the curve of his buttock. It was there the edge of the rock met his armor, wedging him against the floor. She wondered if she could drag his hips sideways into the crevice and pull him out that way.

Clenching his tabard in her fist, she pulled as hard as she could, cursing foully under her breath, but only succeeded in twisting the garment.

He was stuck fast.

She sat back, panting. The only way she'd get him out was if she lifted the boulder off of him.

Refusing to be daunted, she set about measuring her adversary.

The rock was large, as big as the oak chest at the foot of her bed. Its left side nested in the bed of gravel. At the right, it angled up and perched on a shelf of stone. If she could somehow get her shoulder beneath that side and lift it up a few inches...

But it was too low to the ground and too heavy. An ox couldn't have lifted the thing. Even if she did manage to raise it, how would she move Giric from beneath? Lord—what was she to do?

If she only had a lever of some sort...

She remembered watching her father's masons rebuilding the chapel. They'd transported and overturned scores of heavy granite blocks with a system of ropes and winches and pulleys, but the cornerstones they'd levered into place using nothing more complex than a wooden plank.

A wooden plank...a wooden...

Her harp.

Of course.

If she could slip her harp diagonally through the crevice, anchor it against the floor, and rock it back onto its seat, it would lift the boulder. Then, if she shoved the harp forward, the rock would wedge itself into the dip at the top of the harp, and she could pull Giric out.

She plucked the instrument quickly from the floor, but as soon as her fingers contacted the curved wood, her throat closed.

She'd had her harp as long as she could remember. Her mother had taught her to play as a wee lass. Her musical talent was a source of great pride to her father. Whenever she grew melancholy, she had only to pluck out a roundelay, and soon the melody would dispel the mists of sorrow.

She caught one string upon her fingertip and released it, letting its pure, light tone resonate in the cave. Using the instrument so roughly would irreversibly damage it. The stone would abrade the wood finish and possibly crack the sounding box. Yet, she thought, giving the harp a teary hug of farewell, this was without a doubt the instrument's noblest calling.

With a grimace of remorse at the atrocious grating noise, she slid the instrument across the gravel into the crevice until it lodged under the boulder. Then she straddled the harp, gripping the top edge along the highest strings.

Taking a few preparatory breaths, she tipped in counterbalance, and gradually, slowly, she felt the rock give. When the boulder raised a fraction of an inch, she became so ecstatic she nearly dropped it through the floor.

But it wasn't enough. She eased the harp back into place. The base wanted to skid against the uneven floor. If she was going to do this at all, she'd have to be quick. Summoning up all her strength, she delved her heels into the earth at either side of the instrument and joined her hands atop the apex of the harp, grimacing at the throbbing pain in her injured finger. Groaning with the effort, she leaned back with all her weight. This time the boulder lifted at least an inch, and using one foot, she kicked the base of the harp forward to wedge it beneath the elevated rock.

The wood creaked in protest at the tremendous weight, and Hilaire gasped. Had she made things worse? Would the rock drop even farther? She dove for Giric's feet and attempted to haul him backwards. There was still little clearance, and she struggled to twist him free, wincing as his chainmail scraped between the boulder and the gravel floor, afraid of what she might be doing to his exposed skin.

The harp groaned again. Hilaire tugged hard.

"Shite!"

He was stuck. Damn the knight's broad chest—his breastplate must be caught. She groped with her uninjured hand along the underside of the rock, seeking the snag. It was the edge of his epaulet. She skinned her knuckles, holding the armor plate down while she struggled to wrench him backward.

One of the harp strings popped under the strain.

"Come on!" She heaved. "Come on!"

She strove backwards, her heels skidding in the dirt. A second string popped. The wood screeched in slowly rising complaint.

"Come...on!"

She scrambled to her feet as several more strings broke, portending the fatal cracking of the harp's spine. Then, just as the instrument gasped out its final splintering word, she managed to pull him clear.

She didn't know if the boulder simply came to rest back where it was or fell further and sealed the crevice. She didn't *want* to know. Either way, her harp was gone, and if she hadn't moved swiftly, he too would have been lost.

But she'd saved him. She'd saved Giric. She mopped her forehead with the back of her sleeve. No longer able to feel her injured hand, she paused for a moment in silent victory.

There was still much to do. His heart beat, aye, but was his body sound?

Curse the dark! She couldn't even see if he was bleeding. She'd have to assess his injuries by touch. And to do that, she'd have to remove his armor.

Giric felt someone disarming him. Perhaps his squire. But the lad was fumbling with the rivets as if he'd never done the task before. Giric would have upbraided the lad, but he couldn't move, couldn't speak.

Then he remembered the accident. There had been another rockfall. He'd been knocked forward and…

And now he was dead. That was it. That was the reason he couldn't move. It must be an angel taking his armor from him, for what need did a knight have for chainmail in heaven?

But nay. The Dire Dragan was not destined for heaven. More likely it was one of Satan's minions stealing his plate.

He lay helpless while the wretch unbuckled his greaves, cuisses, and epaulets, and struggled with his chainmail and hauberk.

Then the poking began. First his arms, then his chest, then along the length of one leg. Someone seemed intent on finding each and every one of his bruises.

But it was the palm pressed with sudden and alarming candor upon his loins that roused him from his stupor. Demons might lay claim to his mail, but...

"What the devil do ye—" he slurred.

"M'lord!"

Much to his amazement, it was Hilaire. With a startled gasp, she removed her hand.

"I...I cannot see in the darkness," she explained, "and I..."

She clearly hadn't meant to touch him *there.* But Giric couldn't help but wish she would again. Already that neglected part of him roused to her brief caress.

"Are ye unharmed?" she asked.

"So 'twould seem." He groaned at his bruised ribs, sitting up dizzily. "What happened? Are ye hurt?" It rankled at him, knowing he'd lain helpless while she ministered to him, unable to come to her defense.

"I'm fine. There was another collapse. Ye were knocked breathless by a great boulder, and I used my harp to pry..." She sighed shakily. "It doesn't matter. Ye're safe now, and ye seem whole. Ye've a nasty gash on your forehead, but as for the rest, your armor must have done its duty, for I felt no broken bones."

He wondered just how thoroughly she'd examined him.

"I'm grateful for your tender care, lass," he murmured, though it was more desire than gratitude his body expressed to him now.

He slicked his fingers briefly across his brow. Indeed, it was swollen and wet with blood, but the cut was insignificant. He'd be left with a scratch and a mottled bruise on the morrow.

The morrow...

Would there be another morrow for them? Was it possible the second rockslide had brought them closer to escape? Or did God mock them by doubly sealing their fate?

He had to find out.

He discovered at once, cracking the back of his head as he stood up, that the ground above the place he'd been digging had collapsed, narrowing the space between floor and ceiling considerably. He had to sidle halfway around the cavern before he could stand upright. Considering the wealth of debris and the fact he'd been standing directly under the slide, he was lucky indeed to be alive. He ran blistered fingers over the rubble and pricked his thumb on a long sliver of wood.

Her harp. Or what was left of it. The thing lay in splinters, smashed beneath a great boulder.

He frowned. What was it she'd said? A rock had knocked him senseless, and she'd used her harp to pry...

Dear God—she'd levered this enormous rock off of him. He shuddered as he realized by the size of the boulder how close he'd come to getting his skull crushed. But, however she'd managed it, Hilaire had sacrificed her precious possession to save him.

A new longing swelled in him, a desire he had little hope of realizing, a desire to cherish her.

Which made it all the much harder to admit the truth. The fresh slide had blocked what had once been their most likely avenue of escape.

# CHAPTER 7

ilaire would be strong. For Sir Claw's—Giric's—sake, she had to be. He'd done everything in his power to save them. She wasn't about to demean his efforts with childish whimpering. But he'd circled the chamber four times now, and she knew he only delayed giving her the inevitable bad news.

"I've heard," she said, swallowing hard, forcing her voice to remain steady, "'tis not an unpleasant way to die." The last word cracked, and she bit her lip to halt its trembling.

"What's this?" he said, and she could hear his forced levity. "Have ye given up on me so soon?"

She groped forward and contacted his upper arm. It was a good arm, a strong arm, warm now without its steel plate. It was an arm a wife could have depended upon.

"Kind sir, I am past false hope," she said, summoning up all the dignity and grace her station had taught her. "And I pray ye won't think me too selfish. But I'd rather have ye here when I draw my last breath than dead from exhaustion hours before."

"My lady, I..."

"Ye've worn your fingers ragged."

"I would gladly wear them to the bone for ye," he answered, startling her with his fierce promise.

Nonetheless, she squeezed his arm. "Nay. Stay with me. Please." She hoped she didn't sound as desperate as she felt. "I cannot bear the thought o' dyin' alone."

He said nothing, but when he cleared his throat a moment later, she could tell he'd taken her words to heart.

"In truth," he murmured at last, "'tis said to be no more fearsome than driftin' off to sleep."

Tears brimmed in her eyes. Though she'd known the truth, hearing it from his lips gave it brutal substance.

"And one as young and sweet as ye," he added, "shall doubtless be conveyed to heaven ere your flesh feels the chill o' death."

"And ye'll come with me, won't ye?" She clasped his arm tightly now, afraid to let go.

"Me?" His chuckle was melancholy. "I fear not, m'lady. A man such as I was not made to dwell amongst angels."

"Nay, say not so!" she cried, stepping close to him. "Ye're a good man." She clenched her fist upon his linen shirt, over his heart. "Ye gave me comfort in the dark. Ye told me about the sea and…and bandaged my hand. Ye bloodied your fingers diggin' at the wall for me. And not once did ye lift your voice in scorn, though ye knew I fled my betrothed. God's truth, ye've been as virtuous as…as a saint!"

He laughed in sincere amusement this time, which only fueled her righteous rage.

"Sirrah, I will *drag* ye through the gates o' heaven if I have to," she insisted, "else I will join ye in hell."

He clasped her wrists lightly in his battered hands, and she could feel the bittersweet warmth of his smile.

"I believe ye would," he said.

He ran his thumb along the palm of her good hand, and she marveled at the way such a well-muscled fighter could gentle his warrior touch. Perhaps it was as her maid said, that a woman brought out the mildness in a man.

But she would never know. For she would never marry.

And that realization, more than any other, planted the seed of cruel yearning in her throat and opened the floodgates of her tears, tears she shamefully spilled all over the linen of his shirt.


Giric melted at the sound of her weeping. Taking Hilaire in his arms was as natural as gathering his cloak about him on a winter's eve. She fit into his embrace as if she were molded for it. Her head tucked perfectly into the hollow of his shoulder, and he could smell the womanly scent of her upon the soft cloud of hair beneath his chin. She felt so tiny, so fragile within his brawny arms that he feared to crush her, and yet she cleaved to him with amazing strength. Her body hitched as she tried to cease her sobbing, but when he brushed the back of his finger across the delicate line of her jaw, it came away wet.

She thought him a hero. The idea was dizzying. He'd done nothing to help her. On the contrary, by his very name, he'd sentenced her to this fate. And yet she looked to him for comfort.

Would God he could save her! But what meager hopes they'd had of escaping were dashed now by the second avalanche. More digging would only increase the risk of a deadly slide. Running out of air was a merciful passing, but to be crushed under a deluge of rock... Nay, the best he could do was to try to make her last moments as painless as possible.

He slowly traced her backbone with his palm. She was slender, this betrothed of his, with the subtle curves of a young woman. It was a travesty she'd never see the other side of twenty.

He gathered her hair in his other hand, brushing it back from her damp cheek. It was soft as rose petals, thick and possessed of a sleek curl that was wont to curve about his hand. How odd, he thought—he'd no notion of its color.

"I'm sorry. I'm tryin' to be brave." She said it so quietly, he thought he imagined the words. "'Tis only that there were so…so many things I'd yet to do…and now…"

She stifled her sobs as best she could.

He cradled the back of her head and tried to remember what it was like to be so young, like an arrow nocked for the firing, to have a lifetime of adventure stretching out its hand and the bright blue promise of the open sky above.

Lord Giric mac Leod had had his adventure. The Dire Dragan had fought for his King, traveled abroad, won a castle, wed not once, but thrice, served his fellow man as best he could. If he lacked that one elusive hallmark of achievement, an heir to carry on his title, still it couldn't be said he would die before he'd tasted life.

But Hilaire…

He enfolded his arms more tightly about her, enveloping her in all the solace he could extend. She didn't deserve to die. Curse fate—she didn't deserve this.


Hilaire rested her head against Giric's chest. His arms felt wonderful around her. Which made her all the more miserable.

Without chainmail, his embrace this time was far more intimate. She felt the flex of his muscles as he

tightened his hold and the warmth of his skin where her forehead touched his collarbone. He smelled like leather and spice, utterly masculine and irresistibly intriguing.

She closed her eyes, soaking in the scent of him, the feel of him, memorizing his essence, longing to carry the impressions with her into eternity. For it was all she'd ever have of him, all she'd ever know of any man.

She grieved in silence. His knuckles grazed her cheek, collecting her tears, and yet he never shrank from her. How noble he was, she thought, how chivalrous and honorable and kind.

She rubbed her cheek against his hand. His fingers were ragged but warm with life, and on impulse, she turned her head to rest her open lips against them. Without thought, without invitation, she kissed the back of his hand, closing her lips tenderly over each skinned knuckle. A curious addiction came over her, and she found, like dining on sweetmeats, she could not stop. Again and again she pressed her mouth to his flesh, until she heard him groan.

Lord—she hadn't meant to injure him.

He didn't pull away. But he turned his hand over and stopped her, crossing his palm over her parted mouth.

"Did I hurt ye?" she whispered against his hand.

He sighed. "Nay." His low chuckle confused her. "Nay. Not with those soft lips." He brushed his thumb across her mouth, and she felt a peculiar tingling go through her body, as if he'd touched her soul.

It left her feeling reckless and brazen and strangely giddy. There was nothing left now, she realized. No one to answer to. No one to judge her. Why not cast caution to the wind?

"Kiss me," she murmured.

"What?"

"Kiss me." Even the heat that rose in her cheeks couldn't prevent her rash plea. "I've never been kissed before. Please...kiss me."

His breath collapsed out of him, blowing tendrils of her hair back. "Ye want me to...ye want *me* to..."

"Aye, kiss me." He was stone silent, and a shiver of worry rocked her. "Unless ye find the thought distastef—"

His hand slipped aside, replaced so quickly by his mouth she hadn't time to draw breath. And suddenly she floated on a wave of sensation like she'd never felt before.

His chin was rough and foreign to the tender skin of her face, but so distracted was she by the startling softness of his mouth, she scarcely noticed. He tasted of earth and ale and desire. And the way his lips clung to hers, tugging, drawing, calling to her, she cared for nothing but responding in kind. It was heaven, this kissing, and she wished it would never end.

Then he opened her lips with his, and the liquid heat of his tongue teased at the edges of her mouth before sliding in to brand her own tongue. As if she bore his scorching mark, she writhed against him, and a hot bolt of lust shot through her, sizzling her very bones.

His hands cupped her face then, steadying her, thank God, for she feared she might well collapse under his onslaught. He tasted like fiery nectar, and she longed to drink and drink until she grew besotted upon his kiss.

Her ears were still thrumming, her body vibrating like a harp string, her heart racing when he slowed his kisses and drew gradually away from her.

She should have been sated. She knew that. He'd given her what she'd asked. Why then did she hunger for more?

Why did she crave him as keenly as a starving man craved meat?

Why did every nerve in her body sing with current, as if the west wind whipped up a storm in her soul?

She had no answer, nor was it her intent to wonder long. Casting off modesty like a stifling cloak, she snagged her fingers in his shirt and hauled him back to her.

She behaved like a wanton. She knew she did. But it didn't matter. It was her last day on earth. Her last chance for love. And she refused to succumb to death's sleep until she'd wrung every last drop she could from life.

Giric had never felt so clumsy in all his years. It wasn't the dark that crippled him, but rather the maelstrom of emotions coursing through his mind. Here he was, buried under tons of earth, both feet in the grave, no hope in sight, his miserable life near its end. Yet his spirit soared with ecstasy.

Blood long tepid now simmered and pulsed through his veins. Desires long dormant awakened. His mouth still tingled from her kiss, the kiss he'd found nearly impossible to end. But he'd let her go, the way a falconer must let his prize tiercel fly. And, miraculous as it seemed, she'd returned to him. Now his senses centered on the delicate woman who seized him with all the strength of a knight reining in a warhorse.

She kissed him fiercely, hungrily, and the pressure of her sweet lips sent a frisson of desire straight to his loins. Lord—she knew not in what perilous sport she engaged. It had been months since he'd lain with a woman. With the slightest bit of encouragement, he might burst like a keg of overripe ale. But the way she urged him on him now—it was akin to hefting a battle-ax at the barrel.

Still, somewhere within his lust-fuddled brain he remembered he was a knight, a gentleman, a noble sworn to protect ladies, not seduce them. And if it killed him, he wouldn't violate this woman's trust.

She explored his face now, sliding a fingertip along the crest of his brow, sweeping the bristled hollow of his cheek with her thumb, smoothing the flesh across his jaw, then plunging her hand into the curls at the base of his neck. She sighed against his lips, and her breath was the breath of life, of spring, of sunlight in the dark.

She couldn't know how exalted she made him feel. In the blinding black, she embraced him, accepted him as if he were that man he'd thought lost so long ago. She neither shrank from him in horror nor shook her head in pity, and for once, he reveled in blessed anonymity.

Her fingers coursed along the strained cords of his neck, over the vein pulsing madly in his throat, and he swallowed hard beneath her touch. She nuzzled his ear, her lips nibbling at the lobe, her breath tickling the whiskers along his jaw, and he sucked a tight breath between his teeth.

He wanted her. Urgently. Needed her. He hardened like a molten sword plunged into snow. Surely she felt him stiffen against her, felt the blatant proof of his desire. And yet she didn't retreat. Nay, she pressed even closer, torturing him with her tender woman's shape, letting her hands roam at will over his shoulders, his arms, his chest, so close to his heart.

Hilaire hardly recognized the brazen woman she'd become. She was wanton, wild, and unbridled, like a mare quartered with a rutting stallion. She knew no shame, only greed. For what, she was uncertain. But she couldn't keep her hands from roving over the masculine curves and hollows before her. And if lips followed where hands led, it was with an overwhelming thirst that found no quenching.

He swiftly hardened against her belly like a dagger, and though her cheeks burned at the sensation, for she knew well the significance of his swelling, she felt no desire to withdraw. In truth, she longed to press even nearer his man's body, to lose herself in his arms, in his lust, in his power.

A vibration sang along her spine like the sounding of her harp, humming in her ears, reverberating low in her belly, until it emerged on a moan from her throat.

He answered at once, a groan edged with animal heat, and her passion flared like dry boughs tossed onto flame, turning her to a burning pillar of longing. She needed...needed...

Him.

His arms.

His mouth.

Closer.

With a stranger's hands, she clawed at his garments, willing them gone, whimpering against his mouth when they wouldn't obey her.

And then he caught her fists against his heaving chest, halting them, gasping as he grunted a warning. "Nay...ye must not."

"But I want... I need..."

His hot breath seared her fingers. "Go now. Back away. Before I forget I am a gentleman."

But she was beyond caring. "Nay. I want... I want..."

She knew what she wanted, but mere words could not express her desire. So she pulled her hands from his and rapidly began loosening the laces of her kirtle. It was a wicked thing, displaying her lust like a common tart, and yet no pang of regret afflicted her.

When she had loosed her garment, she took his hand in both of hers and, kissing his palm, placed it where she wanted it most, upon the tingling curve of her bosom.

He gasped as if burned, but she held his hand there, thrilling to the sensation of the rough pads of his fingers upon her untried flesh.

"Lady, ye know not what ye do...what ye..."

She slipped his hand further inside her bodice, sighing in pleasure at the way his fingers curved perfectly about her breast, as if they were made for just such a thing.

"Ah, God," he cried, and the hunger in his voice incited her to a fever pitch of longing.

She lunged against him, and his hand moved fully over her, his fingers brushing the sensitive peak. She drew in a sharp breath, catching her bottom lip between her teeth, so aching sweet was the sensation. Nothing could possibly feel more divine, she thought.

Until he lowered his head, tickling the flesh of her bared shoulder with his thick hair, and closed his lips over the crest of her nipple.

Giric knew better. He knew if he dared to taste her, if he dared slake his thirst, it would be his undoing. Yet her own reckless abandon, her wantonness, her encouragement, compelled him onward. So, despite dire misgivings, he knelt to savor her ambrosia on his starving tongue.

"Aye. Oh, aye," she groaned, firing his blood till he shook with an ecstasy of longing.

Her breast's twin was just as succulent, and she moaned softly as he took his pleasure there as well, laving the supple flesh to a stiff peak.

She tangled her fingers in his unruly locks, holding him to her, accepting him, and his heart soared even as his braies swelled to bursting.

"Oh, God." Her sigh ruffled his hair. "Please..."

It was as if she spoke directly to that appendage between his legs, for it responded as if it knew for what she begged.

But here he had to intervene. Here he had to curb his animal desires and muster strength to prevent them both.

"We mustn't..."

"Please," she whispered.

"But my lady, I fear…"

Her fingers found his lips. "Do not fear. Do not speak. Only…please…"

His groan was somewhere between a laugh and a sob. Lord—Hilaire didn't even know the words to ask for what she desired. She didn't even know her passion's name.

But that didn't stop her from demanding satisfaction. Or begging for it. She dropped to her knees before him and caught his shirt in her fist. "Please."

He had to draw the words from the depths of his mortal soul, from the heart of his chivalry, and they were dragged from him as harshly as an arrow from a wound. "I…cannot."

"Why?" she whispered.

"Because ye're an innocent," he murmured. "And I am a knight, under a vow to protect—"

"Damn your vow."

He desired nothing more. But Hilaire spoke from that innocence. She had no idea what she demanded of him.

"What have we to lose?" she asked. "What more horrible destiny awaits us if we act on our desires rather than denyin' them?"

He felt her gaze in the dark, and he knew, for all her youth and innocence, she was right. They were bound to die anyway. And no act could further stain his already scarred soul.

"Please," she entreated, reaching up one hand to stroke his cheek. "I would taste love just once ere I die."

His heart melted at that, and he swallowed hard. Then he nodded, and she collapsed gratefully into his arms.

"It may not be as ye expect," he murmured against her hair.

"It doesn't matter."

"I don't wish to hurt ye."

She toyed with the laces of his shirt. "Does not a new-made knight endure the accolade o' his lord's fist?" Her fingertip traced the outline of his mouth. "What is a rite o' passage without pain?"

He nipped at her finger, calmed the beast in his braies, and considered carefully what he was about to do.

Hilaire was his betrothed. She was to have been his. Their wedding would not, it appeared, come to pass. They had no lifetime together then, not years or months or even days.

But they had this moment, now. And perhaps in this small sliver of time, he could grant her just one precious gift—the gift of his body, the gift of his love.

Hilaire would have been lying if she said she was not apprehensive. But as soon as Giric gently began

removing her garments, assuring her with constant touches that he was there for her, her fears vanished like mist. Before long, she stood naked before him in the dark, listening while he disrobed as well.

He lay her tenderly atop the hard earth floor, cushioned by their garments. For a long while he did nothing but run his hands over her, like a potter shaping clay, and by the quickening of his breath, she could tell he approved of her form.

She explored his contours as well, the magnificent breadth of his shoulders, the hard ridges of his stomach, the powerful cut of his arms. He was beautiful, this man who was to be her husband, who *was* her husband, and she let her hands roam lower, eager to know everything about him.

He grunted as she enclosed the warm, firm length of him in her palm. For all the crisp nest of curls at his base, his skin was amazingly soft, and he stiffened in her hand like a steel sword sheathed in velvet.

"Lady," he rasped, guiding her hand away, "ye will undo me. Have patience."

She lay back then, surrendering to his pace, and he brought her a feast of delights. He left little of her untouched, stroking her reverently from the crown of her head to the sensitive soles of her feet. He kissed her belly, and she arched to meet his mouth. He ran his tongue along the back of her knee, and she squirmed in pleasure. He sucked on her fingers, licking the delicate webbing between, and she gasped in unexpected delight.

But all the while an ache grew deep inside her, a carnal hunger between her thighs, and this was the one spot he would not touch, no matter how her body silently begged. She moaned for him, rocking her head to and fro, lost in dreamy languor as he tormented her.

"Shh," he admonished. "Hush. 'Twill come."

At long last he slung one heavy thigh over hers, pinning her, and slipped one stealthy hand down between her breasts, over her belly, and into the thick of her woman's curls. She arched upward, mewling, willing him to touch her...there. And when he finally did, when the moist tips of his fingers parted the petals of her maiden's flower and touched the treasure within, she had to bite her lip to still her cry of relief.

He circled over her flesh then, sliding his hand across her again and again. And he kissed her—on the mouth, on her eyelids, beneath her ear, atop her breast—branding her with his lips till it seemed he possessed every inch of her. For a long while she languished in an agony of ecstasy, and then he murmured in her ear.

"Are ye ready for me?"

His rough voice tugged at her passions, and she answered him breathlessly. "Aye. Oh aye."

Then she felt him move over her, felt the weight of him above her, and she stiffened. But he didn't press down upon her yet. Instead, he moved his fingers with more purpose over and over the aching nubbin at her core. With his other hand, he played gently with her breasts, awakening such pleasure that she felt afire with it. And then, when she thought she could feel no higher joy, a curious current began to build within her veins, amassing emotion and sensation into one swirling cloud of pure rapture.

For one glorious moment, she floated high above the ground, free of care, free of fate, free of her body.

All at once, with a brilliant flash like a thousand bolts of lightning, she cried out her passion on his name, plummeting across the sky and earthward on the wings of a comet.

Giric pressed into her as swiftly and mercifully as he could, but his focus had been irrevocably shattered by her victorious cry.

Giric.

She'd called him Giric.

She knew.

She couldn't possibly understand what redemption she offered him when she spoke his name, but he felt suddenly as if he could burst through walls of solid rock for her.

He filled her completely now, and he sighed at the utter bliss of woman's flesh surrounding him. She made not a murmur of protest while he waited for her burning to ease and her body to relax.

"Oh, Hilaire." He wanted to say a hundred things to her, to apologize, to thank her, to vow his undying devotion. But she moved against him, and all his thoughts were lost as desire surged in his veins like a swollen river.

A mere score of thrusts, and his long-idle member nigh exploded with relief, spilling its bounty into her hot womb. He shuddered, torn apart mentally and physically by the wondrous woman beneath him. Moved past speech, grateful beyond expression, he simply groaned her name over and over, kissing her face, her hair, her mouth until she giggled with delight.

Hilaire had never felt anything so wondrous. His breaching of her maidenhead had been like the splitting of a chrysalis, birthing a new and brilliant butterfly. She felt beautiful and precious and alive.

This was the magic of lovemaking, she realized. Not only the heady desire and the fierce explosion of passion, but this enveloping glow afterward. He still filled her, and it seemed he belonged there, deep inside, as if she'd always been waiting for him, as if he were a part of her.

She nuzzled his neck, where his pulse yet throbbed warm against her cheek, and, for one miraculous moment, forgot about everything but the two of them.

"I love ye," she whispered recklessly, blushing at her own confession, but knowing she'd follow him anywhere now, whether he journeyed to heaven or hell.

He squeezed her tighter, and his chuckle sounded almost like a sob. "God curse me for a doomed fool, but I love ye as well."

And then, laughing together in the somber face of death, they slowly drifted to sleep, their limbs entwined, their hearts entangled.

They'd thrown down a gauntlet, challenged fate, braved despair, and defeated heartache. Now, whether they stormed the gates of heaven or were damned to the fires of hell, The Dire Dragan and his Lady Hilaire were destined to spend eternity together.

A trickle of dust awakened Giric. He opened his eyes.

Where was he?

He tried to remember, but his thoughts were sluggish to form.

He blinked.

Slowly, he recalled. There had been a landslide. He'd been trapped underground. And the lass who was to be his wife had been trapped with him.

How much time had passed?

An hour?

A day?

Two?

The air was so stale he could scarcely breathe, his mind so confused he couldn't comprehend the bright white line that appeared to cut the world in half.

He heard voices. Faint, growing stronger.

His captain.

A woman.

Somebody else.

Squinting, he realized the line was a beam of sunlight.

Rescue. It was rescue.

Campbell had found them. His men and the lady's, from the sound of it, were breaking through the wall of rubble.

His heart leaped in his breast. He turned to jostle Hilaire awake, to tell her the miraculous news.

"Hilaire!" he croaked, his throat as dry as dust. He shook her by the shoulder. "Hilaire!"

The light was dim, yet bright enough now to make out her features. Her hair was dark and lush, and her face, though smudged with dirt, was as lovely as an angel's. Her lashes fell thick upon her pale cheek, and her mouth possessed a natural upward curve, even in sleep, as if she dreamt only of happy things. Lord—his betrothed was beautiful.

"Hilaire! Wake up!" He shook her more roughly. "Hilaire!" But she wouldn't budge. "Hil—"

Mother of God.

Nay.

It couldn't be.

His face crumpled, and his heart knifed painfully in his chest.

It *couldn't* be. God could not be so cruel, could he? She couldn't be...dead. Not now. Not after all they'd been through.

Yet how else had it ever been for The Dire Dragan? Had he really believed he could break the curse? Had he truly expected salvation?

Anguish seeped into his veins like bitter poison. He smoothed the tresses back from his angel's forehead and clasped her limp hand. Her image blurred in his tearing eyes, and he cursed the cruel Fates that had let her die without taking him as well.

A warm, wet drop fell upon Hilaire's cheek, and her eyes fluttered open.

Where was she?

The light was gray, and a stranger bent over her, his face concealed by a fall of dark, unruly hair.

She frowned.

The poor man was weeping. Horrible sobs racked his chest and slumped his shoulders.

Her heart went out to him instantly. Though her throat felt thick with sleep, she managed a whisper. "Good sir, what's wrong?"

His gaze flew to her with such intensity that for an instant she was petrified. But in the next heartbeat, she remembered everything—the siege, The Dragan, the passion they'd shared.

This must be Giric mac Leod.

Her betrothed.

The man she'd vowed to marry.

This—dear God—devastatingly handsome man with sad eyes and a tousled mane, an expressive mouth and a bristled jaw, was her husband-to-be.

She could see him. Every bit of his watery gaze, battered face, dazzling smile, and bare body. Which meant there was light in the tunnel.

"Sweet Mary," she croaked, struggling to her elbows. "We're goin' to get out, aren't we?"

"We are."

The curse of The Dire Dragan was broken at last.

And she was going to be the wife of...

Lord—he was breathtaking when he looked at her like that.

She flashed him a shy smile, and his eyes twinkled in return. But it was all the exchange they had time for.

By the Rood—here they sat, as naked as newborns, and already Hilaire heard her father commanding Giric's men to make haste with the tunnel.

# EPILOGUE

Giric tucked his infant son deeper into the crook of his arm, shielding wee Morgan from the icy spray drenching the deck of the ship. Hilaire laughed again in delight, reveling in the mist, shivering as the sea rose up to spit playfully at the vessel rollicking across its bosom.

"Ye'll be soaked by the time we reach port!" Giric warned.

"I don't care!" she cried, grinning with excitement just before a wayward splash careened off the bow and doused her, plastering her hair to her head. She shrieked in alarm, but refused to give ground. Instead, she raked her hair back from her face, gripped the rail, and braced herself for another onslaught.

Riding the sea was the most exhilarating, thrilling, heart-tripping sensation she'd ever...

Nay, she thought. There was one thing more rousing. She glanced sideways at her husband, who stared at her with an expression of such adoration that it took her breath away. Abandoning her play, she swallowed hard and ambled toward him.

"Ye know," she murmured, running a finger along his arm, "if ye don't stop lookin' at me like that, I might have to pleasure ye here on the deck in plain view o' the other passengers."

His reply was part chuckle, part groan.

She took the babe from him, careful not to drip on wee Morgan's sweet, slumbering face, and nestled back into her husband's protective arms. He made no protest as she rested her wet head against his broad shoulder.

The ocean was just as he'd described, wide and open and endless. It shimmered azure under the cloudless sky, shifting and folding like liquid samite, winking at her where the sun tickled its crests. The crisp breeze whipped at the ship's sails and left its briny flavor in her hair and on her lips.

Wood and ropes and chains creaked in complaint as the ship rocked with the current, but Giric assured her they'd make the journey to France in one piece. And from there, who could say where they'd go? After their harrowing escape from beneath the earth, neither of them desired to be confined again.

Now that peace had been made between their two kingdoms—at least for now—Giric was eager to show Hilaire the world and all the open sea she could endure.

It sounded marvelous, voyaging to exotic places, breathing the air of foreign climes, sailing at the whim of the wind. But Hilaire rather enjoyed being the wife of The Dragan and the lady of her own keep. Giric had given her a new harp as a wedding gift, and she had regaled his vassals with many songs extolling the virtues of her husband. Nay, Hilaire had all of the world she desired beside her.

The babe fussed in his sleep, and she bent to him, hushing him with a tender promise. Then she pressed her chilled ear against her husband's warm chest, listening for his steady, strong heartbeat. He sighed in pleasure, and his contentment rumbled all through her.

This—this was all she needed. All she'd ever need.

Her Giric. Once cursed, now blessed. And the precious son born of their love, the son who would one day find his own lady love among the illustrious warrior daughters of Rivenloch.

Hilaire turned her back on the ocean and burrowed into Giric's welcome embrace. Her love for him was as free and enormous and eternal as the sea.

## The End

*See what's next in*
**The Warrior Daughters of Rivenloch**

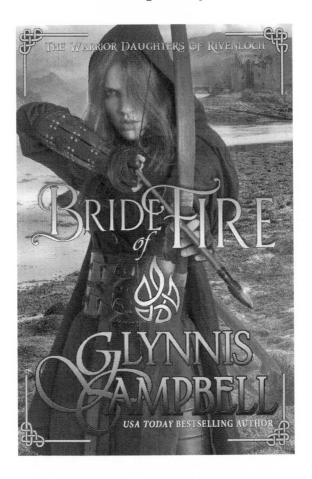

Eager to keep reading? A sneak peek of BRIDE OF FIRE, Book 1, appears at the end of this book.

# CHANK YOU FOR READING MY BOOK!

Did you enjoy it? If so, I hope you'll post a review to let others know! There's no greater gift you can give an author than spreading your love of her books.

It's truly a pleasure and a privilege to be able to share my stories with you. Knowing that my words have made you laugh, sigh, or touched a secret place in your heart is what keeps the wind beneath my wings. I hope you enjoyed our brief journey together, and may ALL of your adventures have happy endings!

If you'd like to keep in touch, feel free to sign up for my monthly e-newsletter at www.glynnis.net, and you'll be the first to find out about my new releases, special discounts, prizes, promotions, and more!

If you want to keep up with my daily escapades:
Friend me at facebook.com/GlynnisCampbell
Like my Page at bit.ly/GlynnisCampbellFBPage
Follow me at twitter.com/GlynnisCampbell
And if you're a super fan, join
facebook.com/GCReadersClan

*Excerpt from*

# BRIDE OF FIRE

The Warrior Daughters of Rivenloch Book 1

### *Rivenloch, The Borders, Scotland*
### *Autumn 1155*

The servants had worked hard to make a home for him here. In his bedchamber, a modest peat fire already burned on the hearth. His chair sat beside it, fitted with a feather pillow embroidered with his initials. His personal things were arranged on the table against the wall—his whale bone comb, a pen and parchment, a pitcher of water with a basin, a candle, a cake of soap, a mirror of polished steel.

He picked up the mirror and winced at the bruised and battered face looking back at him. His swollen eye had a black ring around it. His lip was cut. His stubbled jaw was red and abraded. And at the top of his brow, near the hairline, swelled the lump of a bruise.

He hadn't looked so fearsome and pathetic at the same time since he'd engaged in his first tournament melee as a youth.

He'd meant to introduce himself to his neighbors on the morrow. But that seemed unwise now. He was a mess. He didn't relish turning up at the neighbors' doors, looking like a wildcat that had lost a fight with a wolf.

He replaced the mirror and went to stir the fire to life. Then he lit the candle from the flames, bringing the rest of the chamber to light.

The bed was assembled and made up with linens, bolsters, an embroidered wool coverlet, and sheepskins.

But as he looked at the pair of pillows gracing the bed, he felt a sudden, sharp, unexpected pang, like a dagger stabbed in his heart.

This bed—this chamber—was meant for the laird and his *lady*. It was too imposing and extravagant for one man alone.

She should have been here.

Alicia should have been here.

Sleeping beside him.

Sharing his chamber. His castle. His life.

Choking down his grief, he crossed the room to place the candle in the wall sconce. As he passed by the open window, his eye caught on something outside.

The image was so fleeting, he was sure he'd imagined it.

Just past the window, he stopped in his tracks.

The candle flickered in his trembling hand.

For one terrible instant, he would have sworn he'd seen her standing beyond the fence. Alicia. His dead wife.

Emotions coursed through him as swiftly as lightning. Shock. Disbelief. Wonder. Relief. Longing. Anguish. Misgiving. Dread.

His heart pounded as he continued to stare blankly at the empty black sconce on the white plaster wall, trying to make sense of what he'd just glimpsed.

His eyes must be playing cruel tricks on him. What he'd seen couldn't be Alicia. Alicia was dead. He'd laid her in earth himself. And only fools believed the dead returned as ghosts.

Nay, what he'd seen was likely only a sapling blowing in the wind.

Taking a steadying breath, he slowly backed to the window again and peered out.

Alarm sucked the spit from his mouth.

It wasn't his imagination.

It wasn't a sapling.

It was a lass.

The sight of her challenged his grasp on reality. Her veil swirled around her like a misty aura, glowing from the light of the full moon.

He'd never believed in ghosts. But he had to admit he'd never seen anything look so ghostly.

If he'd seen the figure more clearly the first time, he would have recognized at once it wasn't Alicia. The lass might be enveloped in a filmy white shroud, but beneath the sheer veil her naked body was quite visible.

Unlike slim Alicia, this lass possessed voluptuous curves. Unlike Alicia with her tightly braided black hair, this lass had gold-burnished waves that cascaded down her shoulders. And there was no way shy Alicia, even as a ghost, would have stood naked in the middle of a field.

He narrowed his eyes and studied her.

She stared back at him, unmoving. A gust of wind teased at her veil, revealing long, shapely legs and a delicate dark patch where they joined her body.

The sight caused an unwelcome twinge in his trews.

Still she didn't move.

He lowered a dubious brow.

Perhaps the lass was frozen solid.

Another breeze lifted the veil higher, exposing full breasts tipped by nipples as tempting as cherries. A groan caught in his throat as the twinge grew into a definite swelling.

Then guilt struck him like a blacksmith's hammer, overriding his desire. How could he be aroused when he'd just lost his wife? How could he even *look* at another lass?

Self-disgust tested his temper.

He wanted the lass gone. Now.

"What do ye want?" he yelled down impatiently.

She slowly raised a straight arm to point at him and intoned in a husky moan, "Yooouuu. Muuuuust. Goooooooooooo."

Her sinister directive would have sent chills up the spine of a lesser man. But he knew very well she was mortal. And when she delivered her message, he quickly recognized her ploy for what it was. The mischievous imp had decided to badger her new, unwelcome neighbor.

He supposed it could be worse. She could have thrown rocks at the windows or hung a dead cat on the fence.

As he continued to stare down at the beautiful, hostile lass, he almost wished she *were* a ghost. It was unsettling to have a naked lass cavorting beneath his window. And he didn't much care for her issuing demands.

He crossed his arms over his chest, unwilling to bend to her beauty or her intimidation.

"I must go?" he called out in unimpressed tones. "Is that so?"

"Aaaaaaaaaaayyyyyyyyyeeeeeee," she wailed, making a slow and graceful turn that gave him an inviting glimpse of her tempting backside.

He didn't want to think about it. "Who says so?"

"Iiiiiiiii d-d-d-ooooooooo."

He could hear the shiver of the cold in her voice. He wondered if someone else had put her up to this.

Perhaps a gang of local whelps had wagered on who would do the badgering, and she'd lost.

The lass must be half-frozen. Surely she couldn't keep this up for long. Sooner or later, she'd decide pestering the new neighbor wasn't worth the price of becoming an icicle.

"Ye do?" he asked. "And just who do ye think ye are?"

"A ghoooooooooooooost."

As she lifted her arms, a gust of wind plastered the veil to her body, outlining the seductive curve of her waist.

Desire made him lose his words for a moment. Finally he managed to shout back, "Nobody warned me Creagor was haunted."

"Ohhhh, aaaayyyeee," she cried, waving one arm toward the forest. "Byyyyyyyyyy maaaaaaaaaany ghoooooooosts."

If he weren't so tired . . . and battered . . . and inappropriately aroused, he might have found her performance amusing.

She lowered an accusing finger at him again. "Yooouuu. Muuuuust. Go—"

"I heard ye the first time," he bellowed back, closing one of the shutters. "Well then, carry on! Just see ye don't freeze to death. I don't want to wake in the mornin' to the sight o'—"

A wail interrupted him.

This time it wasn't the lass.

It was his bairn.

For some unfathomable reason, the nursemaids had decided to keep his son in the chamber adjoining his.

He grimaced. No doubt his shouting and the lass's moans had awakened the child.

He muttered a curse under his breath. Then he opened the shutter again and snarled at the lass, "See what ye've done, ye whelp? Off with ye now! Go!" He shooed her with a gesture.

She didn't shoo. Instead, she planted her hands on her hips and shouted back at him in a decidedly unghostly voice.

"Me? You're the horse's arse bellowing out the window!"

Her insult added fuel to the fire of his ire. How dared she call him names? And in his own home?

"Och, that's a bonnie thing!" he yelled. "Cursin' in front of a bairn!"

"Is that what that wailing is?" she challenged, flipping the veil back to reveal her lovely, smirking face...and her infuriatingly breathtaking naked body. "I thought 'twas one of your soldiers, crying for his ma."

It took a moment for the slight to sink in, so distracted was he by the lass's unabashed beauty.

But when her words registered, accentuated by the heightened screaming of his son next door, such fury boiled up in him that he swore steam hissed from his ears.

He wasn't worried about the bairn. Bethac would see to his needs.

But someone had to put that wicked-tongued lass in her place.

He slammed the shutters, snatched up his claymore, and headed for the door.

With any luck, she'd be gone by the time he got downstairs.

If she was foolish enough to stand her ground, she'd flee once she caught sight of Morgan Mor mac Giric charging toward her with his sword. There was a reason for the "Mor" title. Aside from the golden giant Colban, no one in the clan matched Morgan for height, might, and muscle.

One glimpse of him, and she'd scurry off like a frightened coney.

"Shite," Jenefer bit out as the Highlander slammed the shutters and disappeared from the window.

Now she'd done it. The brute was coming downstairs. Which would have been fine if she were closer to her longbow.

But she'd left it in the trees. After all, what ghost carried a bow and arrows? Now it would take her too long to fetch.

Damn her cousins! She never should have listened to them. She'd always said this should be a battle of arms, not of wits. The Highlander hadn't been convinced for one moment that she was a ghost.

What she wouldn't give to have her bow—nocked and primed—in her hands right now.

Of course, bow or not, she wasn't about to run. Only cowards ran away from a fight. So she tossed off the veil, which would only get in the way. Then she blew into her icy hands and bounced up and down on her toes, hoping to warm up her blood enough to put up a good fight.

The babe upstairs was still carrying on. Its wails of woe sailed on the wind, almost as piercing as the cold. She wondered why its mother wasn't seeing to it. Then again, knowing the barbaric Highlanders, they probably toughened up their babes by letting them cry.

Sooner than she expected—had the Highlander *flown* down the stairs?—the timber gates burst open. What emerged was the biggest warrior she'd ever seen.

The breath deserted her lungs. Her eyes went wide. Every instinct told her to flee.

But she swallowed down her fear and braced her knees for impact, even though the fists she made seemed suddenly puny in the face of the beast coming toward her.

He was a good fifty yards away. But his long strides were swallowing up the ground at a rapid pace.

In a flash, all the gruesome rumors she'd heard about Highlanders streamed through her brain.

They ate live mice.

They slept in the snow.

They fought wolves barehanded.

They drank the blood of their enemies.

Twenty yards away.

Like a thunderhead, he boiled toward her with savage intent and the dark threat of violence.

A dozen yards.

Icy sweat covered her now. She was badly mismatched. But she refused to surrender. Better that she should die bravely on her two feet than cower in fear.

Six yards.

This close, she could see his face contorted with murderous rage and hear his feral growl of warning.

Her heart pounded. But she challenged him with an unwavering scowl.

Three yards.

He swept his claymore up in one massive arm, as if he planned to lop off her head then and there.

Still she held her ground and stared death in the eyes.

A yard away, really too close to strike, he finally stopped before her.

She held her breath.

His blade hung over her head. But his furious face was now marked by puzzlement. It was also marked by signs of a recent fight.

He could have killed her. But he hadn't. And that meant he *wouldn't.*

For an extended moment, they only stared at each other, like fire and ice, at an impasse.

Then he suddenly snarled, towering over her and shaking his blade in an attempt to scare her.

All she had left was the element of surprise. While he held his sword aloft, she drove her fist forward, punching him in the nose as hard as she could.

# ABOUT THE AUTHOR

I'm a *USA Today* bestselling author of swashbuckling action-adventure historical romances, mostly set in Scotland, with over a dozen award-winning books published in six languages.

But before my role as a medieval matchmaker, I sang in *The Pinups,* an all-girl band on CBS Records, and provided voices for the MTV animated series *The Maxx,* Blizzard's *Diablo* and *Starcraft* video games, and *Star Wars* audiobooks.

I'm the wife of a rock star (if you want to know which one, contact me) and the mother of two young adults. I do my best writing on cruise ships, in Scottish castles, on my husband's tour bus, and at home in my sunny southern California garden.

I love transporting readers to a place where the bold heroes have endearing flaws, the women are stronger than they look, the land is lush and untamed, and chivalry is alive and well!

I'm always delighted to hear from my readers, so please feel free to email me at glynnis@glynnis.net. And if you're a super-fan who would like to join my inner circle, sign up at http://www.facebook.com/GCReadersClan, where you'll get glimpses behind the scenes, sneak peeks of works-in-progress, and extra special surprises!

Made in the USA
Columbia, SC
11 November 2019